WHEN WE HOLD EACH OTHER UP

PHOEBE WAGNER

ANDROID PRESS

Published by Android Press
Eugene, Oregon
www.android-press.com

First Printing, 2023

Cover Art by Brianna Castagnozzi
Edited by Justine Norton-Kertson

ISBN 978-1958121160 (paperback)
ISBN: 978-1958121177 (epub)

CONTENTS

For the partner, Andrew.
I wrote this book while settling on the unceded land of the Susquehannock people. I also acknowledge the people of the Haudenosaunee Confederacy—the Mohawks, Oneidas, Onondagas, Cayugas, and Senecas—as well as the other people seeking refuge in this area as the traditional custodians of the land I occupy. I pay respect to their elders past, present, and emerging.

PART I

Starlight guard you; sunlight guide you.

CHAPTER ONE

When I first met Erhent, he killed half the apple orchard. That's how Granmum guessed he was more than a mostly dead body, curled at the gnarled base of my favorite apple tree, his fingers dug into the dirt like roots.

Granmum hefted the pickaxe over her shoulder. "Soul-eater."

I touched a fruit-heavy branch, turning brown with his each sleeping breath. "They don't eat, Gran."

"Steal your soul all the same."

He was taking something from the trees, that was true. A thirteenth rotted in the top orchard row. Looking back, I know he would have chosen that spot carefully, a place that needed healing even as he fled. In that moment then, he simply looked like another Harmonizer here to take and make balance.

I picked a soft apple and chucked it, splattering the bark beside his head.

He jerked, rolled away, and somehow flipped onto his feet, except his balance didn't catch up with him. He staggered and fell to his bum.

Gran raised an eyebrow. She shifted the pickaxe, ready to swing.

He panted, his bright eyes flicking between us. Stories said the eyeshine meant he'd fed recently. "Is this land kept?"

I pointed at the dozen dying trees. "You killed a whole row. You regularly find *rows* of apple trees?"

He flinched, lowering his gaze. "It was dark. I was running, lost."

Gran twisted the pickaxe. "It's time to get lost again."

He pulled himself upright using the tree. Wood came loose in his hand, sponging apart with new rot. He wasn't tall by *their* standards, maybe even shorter than me, and I still had growing to happen. His dark clothes hung loose on his thin body, and gray streaked the hair around his face and ears. Usually, they looked young and fit, so either he was very old or outcast.

He swayed and braced against the trunk. Since it didn't crumble to dust, he must not have truly fed on it, though from his trembling hands, he needed the energy. Not that I knew for sure, really, I had only heard the stories of his kind from Uncle Miguel, along with the whispered afterthought—don't let them touch you. Ever.

He took a deep breath, straightened, and stepped backward. "I'm sorry. I'll balance the orchard when—when I can." His head dipped as if he knew as well as my Gran that he couldn't. She huffed as he walked from the orchard even as his steps slowed from sure to staggering.

I counted down: *three, two, one*—

He collapsed.

While I'd never seen one of his kind so starved, I'd witnessed enough people on their last legs. Gran and I waited. She spun the pickaxe in her hands.

I whispered, "You aren't going to kill him, are you?"

The axe stopped mid-twirl. "Never kill a Harmonizer. He must not be part of the city's clan, but even so, they'll come for whoever drew blood. Balance, always balance." She squeezed my shoulder. "Wait here."

She inspected his body, nudged him. He didn't move, so she hooked him with the pickaxe and flipped him over. He still breathed, the condensation visible.

After a ten-count, she pierced the pickaxe through his coat and dragged him over the orchard hill.

I picked the rotten apples. Some would make applesauce, maybe cider. Tomorrow, I'd come back with a saw to trim the now-lifeless branches. Only spring would tell if the trees survived. We'd collect seeds to plant another row.

Half an hour later, Granmum returned and helped me gather the soft fruit.

"We could take him in," I said. "I have energy to spare. He might help us—"

Gran dropped the apples and snatched me by the shoulders before I could duck. She shook me. "Never say such a thing! There were times when we had to make those deals—give lifeforce and let them feed. You don't! I've worked to make sure of it."

I looked away. "Sorry." My Uncle Miguel had told me such stories, of course, how generations ago, the warming Earth had shed them from the glaciers to feed on all of humanity and our waste, our excess. Some stories said thanks to their touch, humanity had come back into balance with the rest of the living world. But Granmum told other stories, stories of how her parents had made deals for food, water, shelter by letting the Harmonizers feed off their bodies with a single touch. Gran made the Harmonizers sound threatening, but this one just looked weak. Uncle Miguel would say that's when any creature is most dangerous.

Granmum grunted as she stooped to one knee and collected the fruit. "Forget we found him. It will only cause trouble at home."

Back then, home was eleven of us, Granmum and Grandmother, Uncle Miguel, Octavia, and the pack who shared the home: three cats (Sierra, Dusk, Star), two coy-dogs (Serenade and Crooner), and a horse. I'd arrived on the horse four years ago, so I called him Brother.

We'd just come to the woods to pass the fall and win-ter a few weeks ago. Summer traveling the valley had been good, with plentiful foraging, harvesting, and sunny days fishing. We all felt strong. Even so, I loved winter best because the work turned quiet, full of stories. There was more time to make beautiful things. Granmum had taught me to knit two winters ago, and this year, she said I'd learn to sew and quilt. Uncle Miguel offered to teach me whittling and had new stories for me to memorize.

I cradled the firmest apples in the tail of my shirt, but I slowed at the sight of the cave's cook smoke. "Gran, you don't think he's the reason the others haven't reached us?" The first snow had come much too early, but so far, only we had made shelter in the caves. Usually fifty came, the number the elders (handed down from the Harmonizers long ago) agreed the land could support.

She shook her head. "He wouldn't be so weak if he'd fed on so many humankind. Now, you forget about him. We have applesauce to make."

~~~~~~ ~~~~~~

Even if the nightly chores kept my brain busy, my dreams refused to forget. Uncle Miguel, the area's historymaker, kept this theory that all stories are about the same basic thing: a stranger appears or someone goes on a journey. Maybe this Harmonizer was the stranger of a new story.

That night, in my dream, he comes to the cave entrance while I'm on watch, even though it's dream logic since I'm still too young for watching until I turn sixteen in the spring.

He offers his hand—it seems to flicker, sometimes gloved and sometimes bare skin. Granmum says never to touch a Harmonizer's skin because that's how they feed on you. I take his hand, anyway. In that flickering, I'm not sure if we're in the cave or some sort of narrow path, tall buildings on either side.

I struggled awake in the middle of the night, the fire burned low. I'd dreamed of the city before, but I'd always been alone in the dreams.

The watch was supposed to stoke the hearth, so that meant Grandmother minded the cave entrance since she always fell asleep. I used the hunting skills Octavia taught me and carefully, slow as a stretching cat, eased from under my knitted blankets. I clutched one around me and picked up my boots. The smooth cave floor made no noise as I padded to the entrance. My guess about Grandmother proved right. She slept in a chair tilted against a boulder with the cats, Sierra, Dusk, and Star, creating a blanket on her lap.

What I hadn't planned for was Brother dozing in the moonlight. His ears twitched as I crossed the threshold. A nicker made me stiffen. I glared at him, and he nodded his head as if chiding. He knew nighttime was not for riding.

I crept over and nuzzled the side of his face. "I'm just checking on the orchard."

He blustered. I shushed him and tried to leave again, but he nipped my hair. Before I had found Gran, two other traveling bands had left me when I made too much trouble and wouldn't let them eat Brother during a bad winter. Afterward, he kept me alive. I don't remember much from before we wandered the road, hoping for others, then afraid of others. Always avoiding the Harmonizers even though I had no name for the strong, white bodies that patrolled the city's edges. It was only later I became curious about the city. Gran and Grandmother avoided these talks, so Uncle Miguel or Octavia would tell me about it when we worked alone or walked ahead of the group. Octavia was just a few years older than me, but she'd lived in the city before choosing to become a nomad. She'd loved the city but couldn't stand living under the Harmonizers, who carefully controlled the population to make sure humans didn't hurt the rest of the living world. Uncle Miguel, twice Octavia's age, said he stayed away from the city because he'd seen too many people starve—a lot harder to starve in the woods.

I motioned for Brother to come, and he clopped from the cave, each striking hoof making me wince. Only the cats raised their heads, though. Their bright eyes looked so much like the Harmonizer's gaze my stomach fluttered. I shouldn't be doing this. Granmum would know somehow, and I'd get a lecture about how we needed to learn new ways and be like the coydogs who never went off alone, or some such. But Uncle Miguel also told me the old stories said to always give hospitality to strangers in case they might be a Harmonizer looking to see if you lived in balance. What if we'd made the Harmonizer angry?

I asked Brother if I could ride, and he let me pull up by his mane. We trotted through the crisp night. Moonlight reflected off the thin snow, so nothing seemed truly dark. A good night for daring.

I swung off Brother at the orchard. He nickered and nosed the dying trees. They looked worse than this morning, the way hands swell with age.

At the orchard's top row, I followed the drag marks while Brother sniffed the trail. A cottonwood copse waited in the meadow's heart, so I only half-watched the trail, assuming Gran would have left him with some shelter and deadwood to eat.

When I tripped, I thought I must've hit a tussock. Except, he moaned.

I gasped and scrambled back. Brother cantered over and nudged my head.

The black gash in the snow remained still, and so did I.

The cottonwoods were a dark smudge a hundred yards off. The Harmonizer couldn't walk a dozen steps. If Gran had left him here, with no shelter and nothing his kind could eat... she'd meant for him to die.

I'd seen Gran kill before. A mountain lion that wouldn't leave us alone, a rabid coyote, deer when the herds swelled too large. Once, a person. A group of men had come, searching for minerals. We expected the Harmonizers to stop them, but when none arrived, Gran and Octavia saw them off. But Gran never made violence without reason.

But what reason had this Harmonizer given except for what he was? Yes, he'd hurt the orchard, but he hadn't known. He hadn't come to balance us, and others said the Harmonizers took less and less each decade as the Earth settled. We didn't need to fear him, even if Uncle Miguel's stories still told their warnings. The seasons of starving and loss were balancing, others agreed—for the most part. New stories about the city to the east had circulated the fires as we'd made our way through the valley to the winter cave, but Uncle Miguel had hushed them. Now, so many that usually wintered with us hadn't arrived yet...

I crouched. He didn't move. If not for the moan, I would have assumed he was dead.

I touched his shoulder, then nudged him. When he remained still, I hovered a hand over his nose, and his hot breath still blew strong.

"I'm going to move you to a better place, okay? I'm not trying to hurt you."

I hooked my arms under his shoulders and paused, tense and waiting for him to turn on me—nothing. Gran would have me memorizing lessonstories again if she found out I came back, but those same stories said to help all, from the drought-thirsty tree to the wounded wolf. I dragged him toward the copse with Brother trotting back and forth as if urging me. By the time we reached the trees, I had sweat through my clothes and the cold bit.

I leaned him against a dying cottonwood I couldn't stretch my arms around. Lightning must have struck the trunk that summer because it'd split, half severed to rot in the patchy snow. Stories said the Harmonizers could feed on trees and other living things when needed, even though they called themselves mankind's predator in the old stories. Hopefully, the cottonwoods offered enough.

I wrapped my blanket around him. I could get warm in the cave, but who knew when he would feel warm again.

Brother offered his back, and we went home.

If Gran suspected, she didn't say anything the next morning. We ate hot applesauce for breakfast, then I went to the stream to haul water. Usually Brother helped me, but he wasn't around, even when I called. My heartbeat quickened—what if the Harmonizer had taken him?—but when I climbed into a tree stand, the cottonwood tops stuck like fingers over the orchard hill. He'd have had to eat all those trees and more before he could have taken down a horse quick-witted as Brother.

I lugged the water pails from the bottom of the hollow, careful to keep from rushing or grumbling that Brother decided he had better plans. Grandmother said that rushing through work and life was what crumbled away at the planet. *Everything more efficient, more quick, so they could make us keep going and going*, she'd say if Granmum let her talk about the past. Granmum would contradict and say something like, *There's a time to rush, but you're smart enough to know when that is. Resting, listening, that's just as important.* Both of them had been born after what Uncle Miguel's histories called the Post-Capitalist era, let alone the Turbo- and Petro-Capitalist eras before that, but they kept the stories. I'd learn more about those times when I turned sixteen in the spring and completed my required visit to the nearest Harmonizer city. I'd give an exchange of energy and learn about how our ancestors came together to balance and stabilize the world. Uncle Miguel promised I would meet more storytellers and learn what taking such a title would mean. The city librarians would give me stories to memorize and see if I had any knack for it. If I did, I might be invited to study in the city. I could always learn from Uncle Miguel and other storytellers we met along our trails, but I could learn so much more in the city, even if Uncle Miguel warned it might not suit me and reminded me that the valley needed more storytellers—the city had plenty.

Back then, the words "exchange of energy" meant so little to me. I'd passed the years living and loving the woods and valleys and hills. I'd assumed the city must hold that same kind of love.

I daydreamed of what might have happened to the Harmonizer, if he'd survived the night. Stories said if you did a good turn for a Harmonizer, they were bound to balance by doing you a good turn. Maybe saving him after Gran left him merely balanced the actions and saved us from something bad happening at the cave. I considered ditching my buckets and running to the meadow to check on him, but what if Gran was right about him being dangerous? I didn't want to bring any harm back to my family at the cave.

Winter and the cave had become linked in my mind like creeks and willows. Since Gran took me in, we celebrated solstice in the rocky warmth. Yes, we would find snow in other places, and lately the summer fields had been colder, but the early darkness, the cozy fires, snuggling under the furs and knit blankets—that happened in the cave. There's also the silence. Summer's loudness is special, but the winter quiet soothes me. This crisp morning, I only heard the stream, the slosh of water pails, the *thwump* of crusty snow slipping off spruce branches.

I felt safer in the quiet because when something bad was coming, you know it so far off. Halfway to the cave, a crow cawed, then two more. They burst from a dead oak tree. I paused and closed my eyes, letting my senses adjust.

A thrumming rumble, headed toward the cave. Uncle Miguel imitated that noise when he told stories of what helped wipe out humanity: machines, running on fossil fuels. I'd seen their rusted husks sunk into the dirt, but never a running one.

Since the rumble cut me off from the cave entrance, I left the water and circled to the cave's back, scaling the hollow's slope that turned into the mouth. I huddled behind mossy rocks as the vehicle struggled along the slushy path. It had an open back, almost like a sled. Condensation plumed black and made my nose wrinkle. That sharp smell had steered me from gathering beside plenty of waterways.

One Harmonizer walked ahead, making a path. If he touched a tree with his bare hand, it vanished, quick as a pebble in a stream, leaving a rippling haze of dust and the harsh smell of lightning. Trunks so thick I couldn't wrap my arms around them—just gone. What was left of their life sifted to the ground, finer than sawdust. The Harmonizer's touch didn't even give the trees to loam or to make homes after they fell. I wanted to scream *stop*, but Gran said when someone created such violence, the best thing was to hide, to watch, and not act hastily unless you accidently hinder others.

The Harmonizers climbed from the front and back of the truck, five of them. They wore clean city clothes, not handmade. Their white skin, bright eyes, and height labeled them glacial Harmonizers, released when the ice melted. Uncle Miguel's histories said the horrors of humankind's excess had already destroyed much of what they considered civilization, and these beings from the glaciers broke apart the rest. They culled all animals to what they considered a healthy limit so the Earth could recover. Other stories said the Harmonizers just lived off spoils left behind by the dead. Uncle Miguel told both versions, and let the listeners discuss which version held more truth. Now, I understand how it's more complicated than that, but we storytellers love to look for the simple pattern that makes us feel right, whittle it all down to one against the other.

But what were so many Harmonizers doing here? Humans that stayed in the cities lived under the Harmonizers, but not nomads like us. Once in a long season, Uncle Miguel said a loner or two would come around, like the one in the orchard, but usually they caused no trouble and left.

The tallest Harmonizer sauntered toward the cave. From this angle, the cave lip hid my family, but I sensed them just at the mouth.

He spoke fast, his words stiff and clipped short. "Who leads this little band?"

"No one," Granmum said. "We are a family."

The Harmonizer made a noise in the back of his throat. "Fine. We are here to give notice you are now within the city limits and considered human citizens of Haven City. As new members of the city, half of you will come with us."

A balancing—they were balancing us without even checking to see if we already lived in harmony. Several voices demanded answers. I would have been shouting, too. The city was three days of hard walking from here. We never went closer since stories said young Harmonizers sometimes came past the outskirts and demanded balance for trespassing.

The Harmonizer hissed in their language, and I shuddered, ducking behind my boulder. The sound clawed like shivering stone and cracking ice.

Uncle Miguel, his voice breaking, yelled that we would leave, right that moment, beyond these new limits. Gran and Grandmother insisted on knowing why the city expanded so far—weren't the Harmonizers supposed to make sure we all lived in balance with the land's needs? Serenade and Crooner howled.

Another voice silenced all of them, coming from behind me. A screech like a tree splintering deep in the wood. I glanced toward the meadow, but no cottonwoods peaked their branches over the hillside.

Brother galloped into the clearing, with the Harmonizer from the orchard clinging to his neck. Brother reared to a stop, and the Harmonizer slid to the ground, steady.

He looked so small compared to the others. A foot shorter, thinner, his brown skin still an unhealthy, grayish cast. He stepped into the lead Harmonizer.

"Why have you come to this territory?"

The other laughed, the almost human chuckle turning into something sharp, like pebbles before a rockslide. "Looking for the troublemaker who keeps spreading word of the city expanding." He patted the cheek of our Harmonizer(my family would hate that phrase— nothing was really *ours*). "Looks like my job's done. Don't need you scaring everyone off, friend." He spread his hands as if he wanted to embrace.

Our Harmonizer locked hands with the larger one, grappling. A kick brought the larger one to his knees. Somehow, our Harmonizer twisted, forcing the other into a chokehold, their hands still locked.

The remaining Harmonizers lunged.

I swung over the cave's edge, landing in a crouch. "Watch out!"

Our Harmonizer shoved away. He took a step forward, speaking in a different language that sounded like lightning curling along the edge of a storm cloud, like wind slapping across the lake.

The other Harmonizers backed off. The wounded one scrambled in the muddy snow before struggling to his feet and brushing off his city clothes so unsuitable for winter woods. His hands had reddened as if burned, and he hid them under his jacket. "Feed to your heart's content, old one, because you better be even stronger when I return."

They clambered into the vehicle and rumbled into the trees.

The Harmonizer kept his pose until the rumble faded, then sunk to his knees. I ran to him even as Granmum snatched at my arm.

"He's dangerous, Rowan!"

I crouched beside him, wanting to steady him but waiting for an invitation to be touched, just as my family had taught me. How could Granmum still see him as dangerous? He had strength, yes, but he shielded us instead of threatening to take. He'd even felt bad about the apple trees, when these other Harmonizers turned old trees to dust without a second look.

He blinked and his bright eyes traced the lines of my face, like anyone met in the woods, evaluating. "Thank you. For last night."

I offered a hand. "You made more than the balance."

Someone gasped as his bare skin touched mine, but it felt like a normal hand, contrary to the stories of fingers hot as coals, palms searing skin to ash. I helped him stand.

So close, I confirmed my guess. Unlike the other Harmonizers, he stood a few inches shorter than me. Besides the bright eyes and angular face, he appeared nothing like them, from his dark hair streaked with gray, brown skin a few shades lighter than mine, his soft voice.

Granmum wrapped an arm around my middle and wrenched me away. She hid me behind her. "What do you want, Harmonizer?"

He raised his hands, palms up. "To repay you for the orchard."

"Consider it paid," Granmum said.

Uncle Miguel leaned on his cane as he walked over. He rested a hand on her back. "Hear him out. He saved our lives."

Octavia stepped in front of Granmum. "Thank you, Harmonizer. Would you share the home for the night?"

Granmum hissed something, but Octavia just shrugged it off. The oldest stories said one should always invite a Harmonizer to stay and follow their advice on how to live in harmony, but I'd heard our friends tell of when some Harmonizers came to a home, they took and took to balance what past humankind generations had taken of the Earth. I knew, just like Octavia must have known, that our Harmonizer was not like the others.

He clasped his hands behind his back. "Yes. Yes, very much."

As always with hospitality, we gave him the most comfortable chair, the best food and water, though he only drank, true to the stories.

Unlike the usual nightly meal, we stayed quiet, gesturing or whispering when we needed something. He hunched in his seat, his eyes unfocused, though sometimes, I caught him watching us with barely a smile softening his angular face. As the moon rose, his leg jittered, and each night noise made him twitch. His eyes darted from us to the cave entrance, as if urging us to hurry.

Once the few dishes had been cleared and the kettle set on its tray, brewing chicory root coffee at the Harmonizer's request, he spoke. "You know you must leave. Tomorrow morning at the latest."

Uncle Miguel poured a mug and offered it to him. "Why is the city expanding? We've never had trouble before."

He accepted the mug and murmured a thank you. "Because my kind tell ourselves we are the safety mechanism for when humankind exceeds the Earth, so the more-than-human would survive. But it's just stories. My kind are too hungry, and there is nothing to limit us except ourselves."

Uncle Miguel sighed. "So, it's starting over, just like the stories warned. Nothing learned; nothing changed."

Silence dipped, except for the cookfire's pop-snap. Here, we worked to make balance, but before I found Gran and Grandmother, the road had shown me and Brother that not all humankind believed in balance. People tried to claim waterways or fields for their gain. Usually, neighbors would intervene. The only way to thrive was together, not one above the other.

"Can't we stop them?" I asked.

Octavia laughed without humor, and Granmum squeezed my knee in a suggestion to keep listening before I added to the conversation.

The Harmonizer rubbed his thumb over the mug's lip. "Some of us are trying. Usually the older ones, those of us that lived before the glaciers melted."

Granmum sucked in a breath. "Then you must be—"

"Very old," he said. "Ancient, I think."

Octavia motioned to the family. "Then what would you have us do?"

He straightened his shoulders as if pulling on an attitude. "Leave. Be safe. Tell others to go over the hills and across the river, at the very least. Far as you can from Harmonizer cities, then live your lives with as much harmony as you can create."

"That won't help you," I said.

Granmum hissed at me, but Grandmother elbowed her. "Let'm speak. Rowan's had better sense than you in this one's case."

"Thank you," he said, "but I don't need help."

"Right," I said, "that's why the orchard is half-dead."

He smiled, and his eyes unfocused as if remembering. "I've done what I can to balance my mistake." He stared into his mug. "Unfortunately, you must leave the trees, anyway."

"And what will you do?" I asked.

He downed the rest of his herbal coffee. "Wait here to make sure none follow you."

"Is that a possibility?" Uncle Miguel asked.

The Harmonizer nodded. "Yes, though I think they are more interested in me now. I'm an oddity because I've resisted them."

Octavia leaned forward, her elbows on her knees. "Why help us? You just said your kind don't believe in the balancing anymore. Why cross them?"

"Because what they are doing is wrong." He stood, and his gaze swept over us. He smiled but it was false. "I've fought them before. Trust me, they think I'm an old runt, but they've forgotten how to fight their own kind. None will follow you."

Octavia's hand rested on the knife tied to her belt. "I've lived in the city before. I'm not going back. Teach us how to fight them."

His smile flattened. "Don't let them touch you. Ever." He nodded at me. "Got it?"

"We know that much," Octavia said. "We need more—how did you bring one to his knees?"

He rubbed his palms on his thighs. "I've picked up a trick or two. You'd do best to travel fast, stay out of reach, and if you must fight, do it from afar."

I opened my mouth to ask *how did you learn all this?* but Granmum also stood. "Then we will repay you by following your advice." She started to bow, but he shook his head.

"There's nothing to repay. My kind is in the wrong now, and would do well to learn from you."

Rather than sinking into the quiet talk and planning of the next day like usual, the cave flared with activity. Granmum and Grandmother organized the escape while the others followed their suggestions—what to pack and what to leave, how to load the coydogs' sleds, what we should carry on our backs and what Brother might take, where to run if we were ambushed.

I should have been listening and helping, but I followed the Harmonizer to the cave mouth. Our planning seemed to have calmed him, as if he'd accepted his duty done. The coydogs Serenade and Crooner trotted over, whimpering and tail-wagging. He knelt in front of them, nuzzling them as if they were old friends.

I waited until the coydogs had settled at his sides. "We don't even know your name."

He nodded at the preparations. "They don't want to know. It's better that way."

I grit my teeth. Uncle Miguel's story theory was falling apart. A stranger had come to town, but we were also leaving on a new journey. These stories weren't supposed to happen at the same time. The story of my family and the Harmonizer would never happen—merely two shadows passing in the wood.

He looked up at me. "Eduardo."

I blinked. "But that's a human name."

He nodded over his shoulder at the others. "I was born and lived among humans. I walked the cities long before Harmonizers took control, and to everyone, I was just another human. Not some power meant to bring all into balance. As if I know what balance is any better than you."

He tilted his head toward the stars, so much more visible after the other Harmonizers had destroyed the trees. I wanted to keep asking—who did he call family, where had he lived, how did he learn to fight? I glanced back at the cave, then decided on one more question.

I crouched beside him. "When you saved us from—the others. You took his hands. Why?"

He turned his palms upward and stared at the dirty lines. "I'm sure your family has told you the stories. Our touch is violence. Or it can be. I can hurt others of my kind, just like I could hurt you. The hands and the feet are the strongest channels of that violence."

Granmum called for me to pack my things since we were leaving before sun-up. He was trying to scare me, though, and I wanted him to know I wasn't afraid. After all, I had helped save his life in the orchard.

"When I was on the road with Brother, before I found Granmum and Grandmother, I heard this story about a Harmonizer. They believed in balance, but if they came to a sick place, or a poisoned place, or a hungry group of humankind—they'd balance by giving. To the sick place, they'd give rest. To the poisoned place, they'd give health. To humankind, they'd give energy. They said balancing wasn't always about taking."

Eduardo hid his face by turning toward the stars. "It sounds like that Harmonizer regrets what he did long ago."

"What were you running from, when we found you?"

He passed a hand over his eyes. "I forget how bright the stars are now." That line could begin a story. If he was so old, he must hold hundreds. He chuckled, but it sounded wrong, false. "Lost again." He motioned to the others. "Help your family. They need you."

I backed away, watching him watch the stars. A realization washed over me: he would die tomorrow. Too many would come, and he would die—for us, strange humans who had first tried to kill him.

CHAPTER TWO

After a few hours dozing, we crept into the starlight. The Harmonizer Eduardo wasn't visible, but I sensed watchful eyes. As my family hurried down the trail, I fidgeted with my pack at the cave entrance. I wanted to say something, but fear and exhaustion and the unknown left my head empty.

Uncle Miguel turned back. "C'mon, Rowan." He wrapped an arm around my shoulders, leaning on me instead of his cane. "I talked with him after you slept. He knows what he's doing, and we should be grateful, not make this harder. We're not the first to come and go by his hand. He's been warning everyone in these new city limits."

I let Uncle Miguel guide me to the end of the line. "He said he was lost. Did he tell you why?"

Uncle Miguel hummed. "No, but maybe he meant he was alone. Someone old as him, he's left many behind."

I twisted away from him and paused. "Goodbye, Eduardo."

The cave remained silent in the fading starlight.

For a few hours, we trekked through the morning chill. The pace kept us warm until the sun rose. Usually when we walked, I kept an eye on the woods and foraged, running ahead or catching up when I fell behind, but this morning, I watched my heavy feet. I'd been left behind before, and even though Eduardo made his choice, walking away didn't feel right.

Mid-morning, the first shriek gusted through the forest. Even miles away, it echoed and shivered the birds from the trees. More answered, deep and hollow, like an avalanche high in the mountains.

Uncle Miguel stopped mid-sentence of his walking story. He whispered, "Thank you, Harmonizer."

"Hurry," Grandmother said. "Fast as we can."

My chest tightened. I swallowed hard. A screaming-gust, like wind before a wildfire swept the woods, and dead leaves floated down.

I stopped. The cry made me shiver like all those nights huddled beside Brother, hoping for a home. We'd only hurt Eduardo, abandoned him twice, and he'd only helped us. "What if he's dying."

"For us to live on," Uncle Miguel said.

I shrugged off my pack. "No, that's not what we do. We take people in and help them."

Granmum gripped my arm. "He's dangerous, Rowan."

I shook her off. "How can you say that?" I faced Uncle Miguel. "That's not what the stories tell us. You told me, 'We do not survive because we are the fittest. We survive when we hold each other up.' That's what you did for me! What's the difference between me and Eduardo?"

He bit his lip and looked at Granmum. "It's true. We can't separate ourselves by what feels safe. Not anymore."

Octavia hurried over and dumped her pack, then mine. She began sorting enough supplies for several weeks into my bag.

Her actions made it real. I would leave and help him or bury what remained. My throat tightened and I choked out,

"What does this mean, Uncle Miguel? If someone came and I'm leaving. I'm not following the stories you taught me."

He hugged me. "I was wrong. We are meant to travel like so many others. We are both the stranger and the happener—just as you came to us but now leave with love. So, I have a new theory. Every story grows from love. You are acting out of love, and none of us should hinder that."

Octavia handed me the newly sorted pack. "And love will bring you back to us."

Granmum squeezed me against her chest. "It must, it must."

A deep roar echoed through the woods, and Uncle Miguel and Grandmother called blessings as I ran.

"May starlight guard you and sunlight guide you!"

"May your path follow a river!"

Hooves pounded behind me, and for a moment, I hoped Octavia had joined me on Brother, but he galloped riderless. I swung onto his back, asking him to gallop harder, but he needed no urging.

We reached the clearing before the fear could set in my bones. No guidance, no weapon, no family following. I might as well be food for the Harmonizers that had surely overwhelmed Eduardo by now.

A hundred yards around the cave, the trees had vanished. Only a hazy dust hung in the air. Bodies scattered the ground like deadwood—in pieces. Piles of dust or bits of bone heaped around chunks of flesh. Three Harmonizers had backed Eduardo into the cave entrance. He held a metal rod with a noose at one end, using it as a makeshift spear. Blood dripped off the pole.

Brother veered toward the cave entrance and reared, kicking at the group. One Harmonizer tripped, and Eduardo pinned them to the ground with the metal rod. He stomped a bare foot onto their ribs. When they touched, light flashed, illuminating both their veins and bones, like the strike of a match. The Harmonizer went limp.

The other two glanced between us and Eduardo before running for the woods. Eduardo wrenched up the metal pole and hurled it with more strength than his thin frame promised. The metal rod pierced one Harmonizer's gut, and they collapsed. The other escaped.

Eduardo limped over and stomped a foot onto the Harmonizer's back. At the touch of Eduardo's heel, the flash twisted up the other Harmonizer, even though they still breathed. Eduardo staggered back, then fell to his knees.

I swung off Brother's back. "Eduardo!"

He tried to stand but dropped to his knees again. "I told you to leave!" His voice broke.

I crouched in front of him. Red welts clawed his face and blood trickled from a line across his throat where they must've caught him with the noose. Light trembled from his palms where the skin blackened and cracked as if he'd picked up an ember.

He gasped, swaying on his knees. "I said—to leave. This is my role, what I do. For you."

I gripped his shoulder even as he tried to wrench away. "But you don't have to do it alone."

He snarled. "Do you see what I am?" He motioned to the bodies. "This is why you leave me alone."

I cupped my hands around his. "Balance takes two."

He twitched away, wrapping his arms around himself. "What did I tell you—never touch a Harmonizer."

A warning quiet settled over what had once been a safe place, a winter nest. Now, no trees shielded the entrance, and silence declared it a graveyard. At least, it wasn't my family's grave.

I stood and hooked an arm under his shoulder. "There's no reason to stay here." He let me haul him upright.

We limped to the apple orchard with Brother trailing behind, his ears alert and head raised. I leaned Eduardo against
an apple tree, and it began to wither.

He sighed, his eyes half-closing.

I stood over him just as I had days earlier. "I'm not leaving
you this time."

He leaned away from the trunk, hiding his face in his
blackened hands. "You don't understand, I—"

I shushed him. "My Uncle Miguel used to say there were
two types of stories in the world. A stranger comes to town
or someone leaves on an adventure. I asked him what it
means when they both happen at once, and he came up with
a new theory: all stories are about love." I settled beside him.
"I love this place and don't want the city to take it unless it's
necessary. You must have loved very much in the past, or else
you wouldn't have saved my family, a bunch of strangers."

He sagged against the apple tree. "It's not safe, Rowan."

The tree groaned as it withered beneath his quiet touch.
"Let me tell you a story about what I first remember. It's not
very safe at all. I began on horseback, at least, that's what I
remember when I ran away from the city..."

As I wove Uncle Miguel's theory into my story about a
strange child on a strange horse, their narrow escapes, jour-
neying from family to family until we stuck, only now leaving again—I imagined how, in a few hours, the apple orchard
would be gone, and we would mount Brother, riding into
the hills to warn others, to help others.

Two strangers, going on an adventure.

PART II

The path comes, the path goes.

CHAPTER THREE

I n the early morning, people surrounded us. Since they
didn't try to steal or kill Brother, who'd woken me
with a hoof stamp before trotting off, I guessed their
motives weren't violent.

And, Eduardo hadn't stirred, stretched out by the
campfire's embers. Something dangerous would have him
fighting, unless he felt too exhausted. After we had left
the orchard, he'd rested as much as possible, riding Brother because I insisted. He'd kept his face tilted toward the
sun as we headed for the river, hoping to intercept others
coming to winter at the cave or in the hollow. Eduardo
had barely spoken except to ask if his plan sounded right
from what I knew of the area. The marks around his jaw
and neck still blotched red, and he hid them with a scarf.

All night, he didn't move from that position, even
when we were slowly and quietly surrounded. The stories said Harmonizers didn't sleep, but his breathing had
evened into peacefulness. Maybe Harmonizers as old as
him did sleep.

I followed his example, staying loose and dozing. A fawn in
the tall grass. From the sounds and shift in the air, they'd bar-

ricaded us. The footfalls sounded human, and they smelled
damp and murky like the river.

Sunlight burned off the mist, and frost crisped my blankets. The shapes surrounding us became solid, some sort of
makeshift wall.

Feet shuffled in the frosty undergrowth. A stick snapped.
"Come on, now. No Harmonizer sleeps. What are you waiting for?"

I fully opened my eyes. The walls came into focus: boats.
Kayaks and canoes circled us, their hulls facing inward. People braced them, holding their paddles like spears. Only
Riverroaders had this many boats. They followed the river until wintering on the lake beaches outside Haven City,
starting the cycle over when the ice melted.

Eduardo rose on an elbow. "You did us the favor of not
attacking in the night, so I wanted the sunlight to show you
we are not a threat. Simply travelers." He glanced at me and
nodded, so I sat upright.

No familiar faces peaked over the edges of the boats, but
several of the paddles dipped. A younger person with a red-
dish beard bright against pale skin held a fishing spear, glaring at Eduardo. That glare—the same type of look Granmum had until Eduardo chased off the other Harmonizers.

I pulled into a crouch. "We have a message for you." The
spear-holder glanced my way, body still angled toward Eduardo. "The city is expanding."

A few sharp breaths caught the quiet.

Now, the spear-holder turned to face me. "Is that what this
one told you? Little one, Harmonizers are—"

I stood, my fists clenched at my sides. "I saw it. The city
came for my family. Eduardo warned us." I took a breath, just
like Uncle Miguel taught me. Hook the audience, then slow
down. Don't rush the tale. "We'd just reached our winter
camp when I found him in an apple orchard, nearly dead,
feeding off the trees to stay alive."

The spear-holder huffed.

I glanced at them but stuck to Uncle Miguel's lesson. Make eye contact with everyone, so you don't tell the story to just one person. Use the pauses. "My Granmum thought like you." I pivoted, catching the older eyes. "She wanted to leave him to—to—" I glanced down at Eduardo. He sat cross-legged, watching me like the others. The oars still bristled toward him. "I helped Eduardo. And he helped us when the Harmonizers came to take." I turned toward the spear-holder. "Three day's hard walk from the city and we never went closer, but they said we were in city limits. They wanted to take half of us to the city then and there. No chance to leave, no bargain to strike." I leaned into the words as I pointed at Eduardo. "He chased them off."

The spear-holder let out a low whistle. "Nice trick, Harmonizer." They lowered their fishing spear toward Eduardo's chest. "Take in a kid so we let our guard down—"

Eduardo gripped the shaft below the blade and silently snapped off the top. He stood and tossed aside the head so it stuck in the dirt. "I've seen your community before. You're following the river to trade in the city before wintering on the beaches."

Two people stepped from the shade of a willow tree. One wore a camouflaged helmet, a paddle angled over their shoulder. The smooth handle gleamed in the morning light. "That's the course I'm scouting, Eduardo." The second person signed the other's words.

"Then I request we ride with you." He motioned to the boats. "We've already delayed your morning start, and we can tell our stories along the riverway."

The spear-holder growled something, but the other spoke over them. "We do not deny hospitality. Not on this river." They shot a look at the spear-holder.

The boats surrounding us rolled onto their hulls, and the paddles lowered. The river people stretched and seemed to shake off the tension that had hovered over us as we pretended to sleep. I took a breath and smiled at Eduardo, but care still streaked his thin face. He swayed, and I gripped his arm. He tensed but didn't pull away.

"Should we be going closer to the city?"

He shook his head. "I need to rest. I can't ride again." He pointed at a willow tree by the bank, and I helped him under the branches.

"Are you all right?"

"I'm just tired." He braced against the trunk and slid to the ground. "Besides, you need time. You can't convince them on the strength of your voice alone." He sighed, and his face relaxed. "At least, not yet."

A dozen boats lined the bank, mostly wooden canoes and kayaks, but they fanned out around a log raft. The captain shouted for a canoe to make room for us. The spear-holder tossed two packs from their canoe onto the raft and called out that they'd take us.

The captain, I'd gathered her name was Brook, motioned with her paddle to the spear-holder. "You're with Brand. While you're in his boat, you listen to him."

I crouched next to Eduardo. "Should I ask to go with someone else?"

"If you can change his mind, then the rest of the community will believe us. He wants to protect his family, so he's doing what he thinks is right. Just like your Granmum."

Brand called us over.

"Don't help me," Eduardo said. He rocked to his feet, and I followed. "Will Brother be all right?"

"Oh, yeah, he'll follow us if he wants, or he might go back to Granmum and Grandmother." Sometimes, Brother came with me if I went on a short trip with Octavia or Uncle Miguel, but he had his own sense about when and where he wanted to go.

Brand nosed the canoe so the river just lapped the front. "I'm Firebrand. Brand for short." He tried to smile, grimacing instead. "Either of you been in a boat before?"

Eduardo nodded, but I shook my head.

"You swim?" Brand asked me.

"Well enough."

He clapped me on the shoulder and guided me into the center. "Just don't flail about and you'll be fine. River's calm for now, so we'll just be drifting. Nothing to stir us up."

Eduardo and I sat in the middle while Brand waded into the shallows. The translator from earlier pushed the tail. They swung in, the canoe barley wobbling, but I gripped the edges.

"This is Jyre," Brand said. "She'll pass along our conversation."

Eduardo sagged into the bottom of the canoe. He shrugged off his coat and rolled up his sleeves. Scars criss-crossed his skin, some almost like the indentions of claws or fingers. He tugged off the scarf hiding the scabs around his neck. The burn-like marks he'd received while protecting my family still glared red. He spread his arms over the side of the boat, dangling in the water. He almost looked peaceful with his head tilted toward the weak sun. His graying hair and thin frame tucked into the canoe's bottom seemed mismatched with the Harmonizer who twice chased off others, outnumbered.

Now, it was my turn. Brand was my task to convince. With a few backpaddles, he kept the canoe in place while the other boats flowed ahead. The kayaks darted between the canoes and the main raft like minnows, settling at the perimeters. The captain, Brook, took point and another kayak, its pale wood dulled with river muck, slid behind us. The last kayaker waved a paddle, and Brand let the canoe drift with the rest of the boats.

I'd walked along the river before, but boating felt different. The river swayed and pulled, like when Brother and I rode together, but any time I moved my shoulders, the canoe wobbled. I gripped the side. The river's coolness seeped over the edges, and I tucked my coat closer.

Brand straddled the narrow seat with the paddle balanced on his knees. "Did you kill our willow tree, Harmonizer?"

Eduardo cracked open one eye. "It's not your tree."

"We camp under it every time we come this way."

"Doesn't make it yours," I said. "My family doesn't call the winter cave *ours*. We just use it."

Brand's shoulders hunched. "I said, did you kill it?"

"It had deadwood high in the crown and rot in one of the limbs. I cleared that away. It should survive more winters, now."

In the back, Jyre signed the conversation, her arms resting off to the side. The canoe ahead of us held three people, one person repeating the signs, and onward. Most of the boats had two people, even the kayaks linking up so one could watch through glinting binoculars. Ah, that's what Brand meant by "pass along." It made more sense than hollering over the river's rumble.

Brand nodded at me. "If you're not afraid of him, then why do you care if the city expands?"

"I'm not afraid of the city, either. The area around the cave can support fifty people. That's what our records have said for decades. If the city expands, then that place will be gone."

Brand guided the canoe around a downed pine tree. "Such is the way of the river. It rises, it falls. The city expands this century; it retreats in another."

He wasn't wrong. My family had similar sayings—the path comes, the path goes. Things changed, and to hold on too tight only hurt, but this felt wrong. The smell of the vehicle, trying to take half of us away. Dread had stalked ahead of those Harmonizers.

I adjusted on the narrow seat, trying to look as loose as Brand, but the canoe's quiver as we floated down the center channel made me grip one side. I couldn't relax like Eduardo. "They came in vehicles, and they smelled, like when you come to a bad stretch of water."

"Gas-powered," Eduardo said.

Brand tilted his head. "Those things died ages ago. You can still find them rusting on the banks or stuck in the muck."

"It smelled bad, like a warning. And so loud, like stepping in a hornet nest." Uncle Miguel could mimic the noise, but it would sound silly coming from me, some instinct said. Silly would be right for later, after all this was behind us, and we remembered what brought us together. I pitched my voice lower. "They wanted to take half of us. Right there. Even though they must have known that area could support fifty, and there was only a handful of us." I dipped my hand over the canoe's side, my fingers skimming the cold water, clear enough to see the stones along the bottom, the shimmer of a fish. "We live careful and close with the land. We never stay long so the land can rest after our feet and fires. We repair when we find damage from the old times. We live in balance, but they didn't care about that. They just wanted half for the city."

Brand leaned forward. "Then why do you trust this one? You just said Harmonizers twist the truth."

"Because he fought them off." I wish I could stand in the boat, but I just leaned in to match Brand. "Just like in the old stories, they were so tall and frost-white. Even though they were a head taller than him, he chased them away. And—"

"And let me guess." He smoothed his beard. "You let him take strength from you as reciprocity, just like the stories say."

I grit my teeth. "I've told you. He didn't do that."

Jyre, the translator, spoke up. "Brand, let the kid tell the story."

He grunted and twisted around to paddle a few strokes.

"He came to warn us. He's been circling the city, warning anyone who can leave that the city is coming, and he was almost dead because of it."

Brand snorted. "Of course, that's why he takes in a kid. Can't you see it? He's using you. You aren't that naïve." He nudged Eduardo's knee with the handle of his paddle. "What do you have to say, Harmonizer? You got your kid spewing your story, but we aren't children. We deal with your kind each year. I know. I've paid the price for entering the city limits."

I took a breath, but Eduardo motioned for me to stay quiet. "Rowan helped me when others of my kind tried to kill me." He trailed a finger across the scabs circling his throat. "But you're right. I am dangerous, but I help the land thrive. That's what—what did you used to call them? Apex predators. That's what those predators did. Wolves. Bears. Tigers. Soul-eaters. We balance. Or, we were meant to. When things worked together."

Brand looked toward the forested bank. Ivy had reclaimed a collection of mortared stones and rusted metal. "Humans didn't."

"Some did. Your history is long and much was rubbed away. What caused this was such a tiny sliver." Eduardo took a deep breath and rested his head along one shoulder. "Let it go, Rowan. He isn't listening."

Brand cut the paddle deep into the river. He grumbled that he was listening, but the river shushed him.

Jyre touched my shoulder. "How many days since you left your family?"

"Two days ago." Though it seemed so much longer than that. I'd watched Eduardo protect my family by hurting others, then we'd just—kept going. What if it wasn't worth it? If nobody listened to us because they were too scared of Eduardo, what could we do? I had to turn the story.

She signed to the others as she spoke. "Do you miss them?"

I shook my head. "This is the right thing to do, so there's no time to miss them. I'll see them again, before long."

The canoe eddied closer to the raft, and Brand slowed the boat with a few back paddles. "Have you been to the city yet, kid?"

"A long time ago. I remember running away from it."

"Then you should know. The city takes what it wants. We just try to stay out of its way."

A two-toned whistle pierced the river's murmur. Jyre set aside her paddle and reeled in a fishing line trailing behind the canoe.

"Dead zone coming up," Brand said. "You'll want to take your arms out of the water, Harmonizer."

"What's a dead zone?" I asked.

Jyre wrapped the hook in a piece of cloth and set the line between her feet. "Lack of oxygen in the water, so the plants and fish can't survive."

Eduardo raised his head. "Pollution?"

"Farming, we think," Jyre said. "When the soil gave out farther west, our stories say some of the big farms moved here."

"Excellent." Eduardo shook the water off his hands then unbuttoned his shirt and shrugged off his sleeves. Only wearing an undershirt, more scars showed along his biceps and lined his shoulders, shaped like the welts on his jaw.

Brand shifted in his seat. "What are you doing?"

"Helping the river."

"How?"

He plunged in his arms past his elbows. "By removing the nutrients and decay using up the oxygen. You won't see a change this winter, but the river will change."

Brand signed something to Jyre, and she huffed, but signed whatever he asked to the rest of the crew. A response came rolling back, repeated by each boat.

Jyre smiled. "The others say thank you for trying. Our ancestors have dredged this section of the river multiple times, but we haven't seen it come back to life."

Eduardo dipped his head. "This should help."

As we floated through the dead zone, Eduardo hung over the side of the boat, his arms submerged. The river mostly looked normal, but in a few patches, the dark water turned yellowish and stank of decay. If Eduardo noticed, he didn't react. Some of his pinched look seemed to ease.

After a few miles, we left the hills for a straight stretch with oak and pine groves on either side, and the whistle sounded again. The boats released their lines, and Jyre tossed the hook to trail.

Eduardo took a deep breath and raised his head. His eyes looked brighter, and the redness had drained from the welts along his jaw. He dried his arms and pulled on his shirt and coat. Only his right hand trailed in the water, now. "The river should improve over time. If I can, I'll come check on it."

Brand paddled hard enough, the canoe shot forward. "Easy to ask for thanks for work nobody can see."

"It's not work. Work has to be done; this should have been done."

Brand turned his back on us, facing up river as he guided the canoe. "I guess you earned your hospitality."

"Can't earn a gift," I said.

Jyre chuckled. "Kid's got you there, Brand."

Jyre's acceptance quieted Brand, and she asked me more about my family, how we chose to live with the rest of the world. She'd come from homesteaders a way's off, but it hadn't felt right to her, so she joined up with the Riverroad community.

"Being part of this—part of the river—it feels right to me. We feed each other, play with each other, love each other. It feels like the gentlest way to live." She flicked her paddle and splashed the back of Brand's head. He glared at her. "And these minnows aren't so bad, either."

Brand splashed her back. "Minnow? Then I guess you're a tadpole."

"Then I'll grow into a bullfrog and eat you whole!"

"Unless I grow into a pike and eat you first."

Eduardo held still as they lobbed their insults, as if trying not to disturb a fox in the woods, but he smiled. His eyes softened, just like they had when I tried to talk to him at the cave. I imagined he was thinking of somewhere else, another time when he wasn't so lonely.

A few hours later, we'd lulled into the quiet of the river. Brand fished while Jyre guided the canoe through the channels. The water was high enough with fall rain and the first snow for easy floating, though my legs and bum itched to be up and walking. Sitting in the boat wasn't the same as foraging along the trail, running back and forth to load the wagon with what I found, or pausing to watch a wolf spider until I felt like catching up with the others. The single kayakers found that joy, taking turns darting into the rougher water. They'd flip and twist their boats like extensions of themselves.

Eduardo still settled in the bottom of the boat, his hands drifting in the current. Occasionally, he'd crack open his eyes, look me over, glance at the others, then settle back into whatever he was doing. Eating, I guessed, like Brother taking his time to graze.

He twitched awake in the late afternoon, sitting upright. He looked around, then twisted and plunged his arms into the water, soaking his sleeves.

"What's wrong?" I asked.

Brand and Jyre both backpaddled, slowing the canoe and putting distance from the others.

"There's something up ahead."

Jyre signed to the rest of the group. "There's the broken bridge where we usually camp."

Eduardo shook his head. He ground his teeth. "I don't know. It's something more." He pulled his hands from the water and shook them dry. Brand stared at them as if Eduardo had picked up a knife. "We need—you should make camp. Send a scout ahead."

Jyre signed his words but said, "We have two hours of daylight left. We can let you land, but we—" She shaded her eyes, then gave a thumbs-up. "Well now, I guess the captain likes you. She says to shore."

The boats turned toward a long sandspit before the next bend. I touched Eduardo's arm, and he flinched.

"It's fine, Rowan."

"What did you sense?" "Something is altering the river."

Brand white-knuckled his paddle. "There's nothing up ahead that would hurt us. I've run this stretch of river since I was floating in the womb. All that's left is the broken bridge where we *always* make camp."

The canoe beached, and Eduardo swung over the side. He paced to the captain, who yelled directions for where to drag up the raft. I ran after him.

She brushed back her locs and pulled up a headband. "This better be good, soulkind."

I tucked that word away. It sounded like a more polite version of what Granmum called him, soul-eater.

He clasped his hands behind his back. "All I can tell you is there is something ahead. Not something that's been there for a long time like the bridge. Something being built."

"I've sent a scout, but I'll warn you—you're wrong, and I doubt you'll find a free boat ride tomorrow."

He dipped his head. "Today was more than enough, thank you."

She tapped my shoulder. "Go on and help Brand set up camp. You rode all day, so you're on firewood duty, got it?"

I glanced at Eduardo, but the captain nudged my shoulder. "He's safe with me. Go on." She winked.

I trudged back to the canoe. Two of the small kayaks had been carried over, circling a fire pit Brand dug in the silt.

He crossed his arms. "If you want a hot meal, you better get some driftwood before the other kids get it all."

I wanted to say I'd made plenty of my own fires, but it probably wouldn't look good for Eduardo. Besides, the captain was right, I'd ridden all day. Least I could do was help make a hot meal.

The camp rhythms felt easy and familiar. Children played chase in between delivering firewood to the different sites. Driftwood collected against the eroded sandspit, and the pine and fir along the bank offered plenty of needles and deadwood for kindling. The adults stretched tent lines or hung hammocks, aired out wool blankets, or set water to boil. The elders circled their chairs around the biggest fire and steeped a pot of tea, sharp with dried mint. I coaxed our fire to crackling before most of the others, and Brand shook his head. "If only you could paddle."

Eduardo chatted with the captain while her second gave orders on which boats to repair while still light. Jyre taught me to make cordage for fishing lines from reeds along the bank.

Like my last day at the cave, the peace couldn't last. The wailing came with the sunset. It stretched over the river, a deep, rifting grief. A few whistles confirmed it was the scout, but the wailing grew louder. The kind of sound one hated to hear shrilling through the woods or ahead on the trail because all that waited was a darkness that couldn't be consoled away.

Solar lanterns flared around the fires as the Riverroaders rushed through the gloom to meet the scout. Brand and Jyre told me to wait, but I lost sight of Eduardo's dark coat in the crowd. I counted to twenty, then skulked to the crowd's edge. I didn't want to gawk at the pain—it wasn't my community or my burden to bear—but some instinct said Brand wasn't the only one to distrust Eduardo, even though Eduardo had lost some of his watchfulness.

The lanterns illuminating the shore outlined the scout pulling a kayak through the shallows as another person huddled in the seat. They moaned, clutching a pack against their chest like a child. Murmurs of recognition passed through the group. I couldn't catch the name, but she was a member of another rafting community.

Eduardo edged the crowd, and I mimicked him, easing to the outer side near the woods, bordering the river so the Riverroaders couldn't surround me. If Eduardo was thinking of running, our packs were by Brand's fire in the middle of the camp, hard to reach.

I wasn't sure where I'd gathered this sense of mistrust, but whenever I'd say such things to my family, like how to position our campsite or about sticking together if we passed a group I didn't like, they'd shake their heads and say such thoughts were unbecoming in these times. We didn't have to live that way and shouldn't. If Eduardo acted this same way, then maybe I'd picked up this sense before I ran away from the city.

The paddler's voice echoed over the water. "They've dammed the river—a new dam. It consumed the boats, and the soul-eaters laughed. They took some of us, catching us in ropes and hauling us up when we tried to turn our boats around. Tochi and I abandoned our boat and tried to swim. He dragged me upriver, but one of the soul-eaters shot him. They killed him!"

Several people turned, scanning the crowd, which made me look for Brand. If anyone were going to blame Eduardo, it would be him. Even if it didn't make any sense—Eduardo had stopped the Riverroaders from the same fate. Brand had to recognize that, and if not him, then the captain.

Brand's voice drew my gaze. "When did this happen, Tessa?"

Tessa spoke between sobs. I couldn't catch it, but the response rippled the crowd: three days ago.

Brand swiveled and cut a path through the crowd.

Eduardo strongarmed me aside. "Don't interfere."

"But—"

Brand stood a head taller than Eduardo. He gripped a fistful of Eduardo's coat. "Well, soul-eater?"

Eduardo clasped his hands behind his back. "Release me, Brand."

"Are you going to keep telling lies?" Eduardo sighed. Fast as a fish in the reeds, he slipped out of his jacket and side-stepped Brand. When Brand reached for him again, Eduardo swatted aside his hand and danced a few steps ahead. Brand stuttered and fumed for Eduardo to get back here, but the Riverroaders didn't block his path. He crouched at the edge of the circle near Tessa.

She glanced at him, then buried her face in the bag she clutched.

Eduardo pitched his voice low enough I hurried around the edges of the crowd to catch his words. "—Tochi. A sunflower was tattooed behind his ear, wasn't it? I tried to save him, poured everything I could spare into him, but I couldn't stop the bleeding. He was comfortable, when he went to the next river, I promise." Eduardo extended his hand, palm up. "I can show you."

The crowd murmured, but the captain held still.

Tessa lifted her head. "You helped Tochi?"

"I hope so."

She rested her hand in his.

I'm not sure what I expected—their hands to glow, a burst of light from Eduardo's eyes—but nothing happened. After a few moments of silence, Tessa exhaled and rested her head on the pack. She eased onto her side, her hand slipping from Eduardo's.

Someone, probably Brand, shouted, "Did you just feed on her?"

Eduardo cut a look over his shoulder. "No! I gave her rest." He took a shaky breath. "Her foot is broken, if she didn't tell you."

Brand stormed forward, but the captain signed something that stopped him on his heels.

"Thank you, Harmonizer," the captain said. "You saw what happened?"

Eduardo slowly stood, his hands stiff at his sides. "Not exactly. I found Tochi's body downstream, I think. I tried to help, but..." He shook his head. "I did all I could before they found me, and I had to run."

So that's how he'd ended up exhausted in the apple orchard. That could have been the fate of my family.

I darted past Brand, snatching Eduardo's coat, which he let drag in the dirt. "It's true. Eduardo couldn't walk when I found him. He was barely conscious. He truly gave everything he had." I handed Eduardo his coat, but he lowered his head as he shrugged it on.

"Rowan, they found your family because they followed me. I wasn't sure until now."

"They would have come for us, just like they are coming for the Riverroaders."

"Enough." The captain shouldered past us, addressing the crowd. "We need to move with focus *and* flow. Rest, mourn, be among family tonight. We will set extra watch, and in the morning, we will make our decisions."

The group slowly separated, returning to their fires. The captain let out a long breath. She nodded at us. "You need rest as much as we do. Change is coming, it seems."

Eduardo nodded and guided me toward Brand's fire, leaning on my shoulder.

"Eduardo," the captain said, "thanks for helping Tessa."

He dipped his head. "Of course." He leaned on me as we walked toward Brand's fire.

I lowered my voice. "Are we safe with him?" Some eyes watched us, but mostly people slid their gazes past us like the way one keeps an eye on a coydog circling a little too close.

"What do you think?" Eduardo asked.

"I would keep moving."

"I'm not sure they'll let us."

"Then we keep our own watches—that's what the stories say to do."

We neared the fire, and he straightened, taking his own weight. "You sleep. I don't need to."

Only Jyre waited at the fire, whittling a bone fish hook. "Stew's on if you want something hot."

I offered her some of my rations in exchange for the bowl, but she shook her head.

"You're guests. Both of you." She nodded at Eduardo. "The river's hospitality means everyone eats."

I felt heavy and warm after the fish stew. Even though I wanted to stay awake with Eduardo, I dozed, settled against a piece of driftwood while Eduardo tended the fire. Jyre used a stick to prop up the canoe and slept under it like a tent. Brand didn't return to the camp, but the captain came by, her voice shaking me from near-sleep, though I kept my eyes closed.

"If you choose to come with us in the morning, Jyre will be in the bow of the canoe tomorrow. Brand has agreed he needs some time to reconnect with the river before he is in charge of a canoe again."

"I don't think it would be wise," Eduardo said. "My presence will probably cause you more harm than good."

"I understand. Thank you for the warning. At least we will go expecting change."

"I'm not sure that makes it easier."

"As we say, you'll never float the same river."

Eduardo hummed. "I like that one."

Eduardo nudged me awake the next time, only a few hours later. The moon hung low, a cat's claw hooking the river. Time to go. The Riverroaders would be leaving soon to make up for lost time, and Eduardo wanted to put some miles between us before they reached this new dam.

I waved goodbye as we cut into the woods around the bank, but a younger voice called to wait.

Three kayakers hurried after us, the blunt boats slung over their shoulders. They were the small, playful kayaks that would dart into the rougher waters.

Eduardo shifted forward, angled between me and the riders.

They were young, but not as young as me. The leader was short and solid with dark skin. They pushed back their helmet. "I'm Jana, and this is Mick and Ruel. We believe you and want to help. We know the tributaries and can try to find any communities you might have missed on our way to the winter beaches."

"You—you do?" Eduardo asked.

I grinned. "Thank you."

"We'll tell your story," Mick said. "And add how we met you and how you helped Tessa. Hopefully, it will convince some."

"There will be more than one new dam," Eduardo said. "Be careful. Listen to the river."

Jana nodded. "If you want to reach more people, you should visit the Archivists." They pointed into the woods. "Keep east, until you come to a lake. They have a radio and other ways of sending out messages. We use them to update our maps."

"I've heard of them," Eduardo said. "Thank you."

They carried their kayaks into the shallows. "May you always find water!"

I waved. "May the channels carry you high!"

The boats angled into the current and swung around the bend, fast as dragonflies.

CHAPTER FOUR

We put a mile or two between us and the River-roaders before Eduardo paused. He perched on a fallen pine and unlaced his boots. "You did good, Rowan. Better than I've done before."

I tightened my backpack straps. "I didn't help much with Brand."

"Brand was hurting." He tucked his hands into his coat pockets. "How many stories are still told about Harmonizers? What do you know?"

I stared at the sky cracked with leafless elm branches. Like any curious child, I'd asked about the Harmonizers, and my favorite campfire stories had been legends about Erhent, the rebel who stole from the rich, who united Harmonizers and humans. My family didn't like to remember any of those stories. Those days were mostly done with, they'd said. As long as you avoided the city, not many Harmonizers traveled beyond the limits—what more did I need to know? "There were dark times, according to Uncle Miguel. But there have been dark times with humankind, too. I don't know what makes us different."

We both straightened as something big moved through the woods, cracking branches and rustling foliage. Brother whinnied, and I whistled. He trotted through the pines, his skin still glistening with river water. He dripped all over me as he nuzzled my hair.

Eduardo stroked his neck. "Ride if you want. I'm feeling better." He tied our packs together, forming makeshift saddlebags, and hung his boots over Brother's back.

"That's all right. I feel like walking."

We continued east, up a hill, and I matched his pace, which still seemed too slow. Even so, his angular face was more relaxed, less drawn, and he took strong steps, even barefoot. "What did you do to the river yesterday? You look better."

"Hopefully the river will look better, too. What do you know of wolves, Rowan? Have you seen them before?"

"I've heard them howling. I like it, even though it sounds sad. Sometimes the coydogs will howl, too."

"What would you do, if you saw a wolf?"

"Try not to disturb it. Uncle Miguel says they are important to the world healing. He says how thankful he is to hear them howling."

Eduardo's bare feet whispered through the fallen leaves while my boots crunched alongside Brother's hooves.

"Once, humans were very scared of wolves. They told stories about wolves eating children. Said wolves couldn't be trusted, that they'd eat everything until people starved. They told stories of wolves hunting people even though that rarely happened. So, people wanted to kill the wolves. These wolves had become monsters and nightmares in their minds. And they did kill them, until nearly none remained."

Uncle Miguel had told me other stories like this: about the bear, the mountain lion, the tiger, but also how it wasn't always fear that lost whole species. Some people had done it to the salmon, the lobster, the whale—just because. I needed to learn those stories, too, but they settled so heavy.

"The world changed," Eduardo said. "Where the wolves were supposed to keep the deer moving, to keep the rivers playful and the meadows wild—these places changed. Those parts of the world eroded, uprooted, died. Some people saw what was happening and realized they couldn't listen to the stories anymore. The stories were wrong. Wolves weren't monsters—they helped everything thrive. But so many others only saw monsters. They kept killing the wolves even though they weren't supposed to."

"That's Brand," I said. "He was told the wrong stories and now he's stuck." I ran and hopped over a log while Eduardo ducked under it. "But how do we know if we learned the wrong stories?"

He passed his palm over a hemlock trunk. "I don't know. Be open to changing your mind."

I held a branch back so he and Brother could pass through. "That doesn't tell me what you were doing to the river."

He trailed his fingers along a wide oak trunk. "I was eating, just like the wolves. Trash from a century ago, algae choking out the oxygen, dead limbs on the trees shading the bank, water plants too far overgrown."

I motioned at his bare feet. "That's what you're doing now."

He scuffed some leaves. "A little, but I'm trying to sense our path. I've heard of the Archivists, but never visited them."

"I've always wanted to, but our path doesn't go that way. Uncle Miguel promised to take me when I turned sixteen next year. They have so many stories." I hadn't told my family yet, but I hoped to stay with the Archivists for a few seasons. I wanted to see if their lifestyle was possible: to surround themselves with stories, all in one place, and still give back to the rest of the living world. Some people in our traveling group called them selfish. They asked how it could be possible to run all those electronics sustainably, enough to store the history and stories of several eras. I wanted to see how they did it—and if I could do it, too.

"Well then, you'll have stories to take back to your family," Eduardo said.

We kept a steady pace, if slow, climbing into the hills. The temperature dropped, but walking kept me warm. As we settled into the pace, Eduardo rarely talked. His gaze softened, and even though he chose the paths, he seemed to be guided by something other than sight. With the same careful purpose, he pressed his bare feet to the cold ground, he passed his hands over the trees or drew his fingers through the foliage. There was a grace to it, like watching Brother gallop through a meadow.

I fell into my own rhythms. While Brother walked with Eduardo, I circled them, gathering mushrooms for dinner, conifer needles and rosehip for tea, even some chicory root for morning coffee. I noted as many species as I recognized, the different tracks or scat, the bird calls or dropped feathers, which I'd add to the map tonight, so I'd know next time what to look for.

A dead aspen grove pulled Eduardo out of his trailing, as I'd come to think of it. Across a broken road, the asphalt shattered and crumpled by weeds, the dead trees bristled, ghostly, along the path. Eduardo sighed, his shoulders falling. "Wait a moment. It might still be alive." He dug his hands into the loam.

"What do you mean? The trees?" My family had passed aspen groves like this before, long dead from bark beetles. We'd try to avoid these stands since the dead trees could fall and crush one of us.

He smiled. "This way. Someone protected the heart long ago." He guided us through the skeletal trees, too quiet for a healthy forest, even in early winter. We crunched over fallen logs, sometimes so thick and tangled Eduardo would carve a path with his hand, turning parts of the trunks to sawdust so

we could pass through. He crumbled the wood as effort-
lessly as brushing aside a spiderweb.

This easy destruction is what Brand feared, but Eduardo did it so carefully, out of necessity. Now, I understand
Brand had witnessed this destruction so often in the city,
with none of the renewal that Eduardo knew how to
bring, the balance Harmonizers were uniquely capable of,
but too many had foregone.

Where the bark had shed from the dead trees, the beetle
trails zig-zagged. The twirling, mazelike designs added another texture to the wood grain, and I paused to trace the
paths. "How can somebody protect against the beetles?"

Eduardo wiggled his fingers. "My kind can target them.
Long ago, one of my kind passed through here and killed
the beetles before it was too late."

"Do you think they're still here?"

"No, not for a very long time. The beetles died out
several decades ago, so this aspen has been growing back.
You'll see."

Just as the sunset rayed between the trunks, the trees
changed. No longer dead, limbless poles waiting to fall,
the bright white trunks watched us with eyelike knots.
I took a deep breath as I brushed my fingertips over the
smooth bark. Dead leaves still clung to the branches, chit-
tering at the faintest gust.

Eduardo walked as if following a trail as the aspens grew
denser. In a small clearing just wide enough for Brother
to turn around, someone had made a wooden lean-to of
aspen poles against a boulder. The trunks had collapsed,
but Eduardo cleared them with a touch. Broken bits of
slate circled a small fire pit.

I climbed on top of the boulder, my feet level with Eduardo's shoulders. "This feels like a safe spot." The intense quiet
of the dead woods had been replaced with the winter stillness
of the living world. A squirrel skittered. The leaves quaked,

still clinging in the cold. The trees bent with the winter wind rather than breaking over.

Eduardo sat in the freshly fallen leaves, then rocked onto his back. He sighed. "I've always loved aspens. They're so big." He spread his arms, his hands disappearing into the loam. After a few minutes, his breathing evened into what I thought of as sleep, even though the stories said Harmonizers didn't sleep.

Well, the stories didn't say how much a Harmonizer would appreciate an aspen grove, either. I didn't understand, then, how tired he felt. It wasn't just the past few days, though he exhausted himself over and over in that short time, but the years before. To see the world so transformed—I can't understand that. That is one of the ways we balanced. To me, these places were fresh and new, which scrubbed some of the exhaustion from what he witnessed, I hoped.

While Eduardo rested, I built a fire and cooked up what I'd gathered along with some dried venison from my supplies. I put on a pot of tea and huddled over the small fire to write down the day's notes. I'd incorporate this part into my story when I had to convince the Archivists that Eduardo wasn't like the stories they'd heard. Maybe they wouldn't need convincing since they had such knowledge, but I doubted it. I wanted to ask Eduardo about why most of the stories I'd heard weren't about Harmonizers like him, but he looked too peaceful.

Even the stories about always inviting a Harmonizer into the home hinted at what would happen if the listener didn't. Histories brought out at festivals or to teach children focused on Harmonizers shepherding, or forcing, humanity through the ecological collapse after the Capitalocene. The only stories that weren't traced with fear were the old legends about Erhent, a Harmonizer during the collapse who helped humans. Most of those stories were just told to settle rowdy children by the campfire on early nights, though from the way Gran and Grandmother exchanged glances or Octavia laughed a little too loud when Uncle Miguel would tell the stories on solstice, after a few glasses of peach wine, I was pretty sure I hadn't caught all the jokes, yet. Except for these legends, Harmonizers were harbingers of hard times—drought, famine, illness. They gave warnings, scared us into change, and left with our strength.

Now wasn't the time to question why those were the only stories I knew—that would make him sigh. He still looked too worn to be roughing the roads or just lying in the leaves like he was, but some of the care had brushed off his shoulders. The wounds on his face and neck had faded, and his shoulders had relaxed. Sometimes, after a hard travel, when we came to a campsite where we'd stay for a bit, I'd see that same change pass over Granmum and Grandmother or the other elders we met.

The fire burned low, and Eduardo still stretched in the clearing, a sliver of moonlight slowly crawling from his legs up to his chest. When I felt tired enough my eyes ached, I stoked the fire with the last of the wood and crawled over to Eduardo. He'd stretched out beyond the heat's reach. I crouched, my arms around my knees. In the moonlight, he didn't look cold. He breathed easy but strong, no discoloration around his fingers, at least what I could see above the loam. He'd slept fire-less and blanket-less when I'd found him in the apple orchard, so maybe Harmonizers didn't need to stay as warm as humans, like Brother or the coydogs.

He cracked open one eye, a matching sliver of moonlight.

I fell backward with a grunt. "Sorry."

"What are you doing?"

I scooted back toward the fire. "Making sure you weren't frostbit."

He stretched, crunching in the leaves, then sighed and folded his hands over his stomach, the way a burning log settles into the embers. "Kind of you, but you needn't worry. It takes much more than this kind of cold to hurt me." He raised his head, a leaf caught in his dark hair. "Are you warm enough?"

"I know how to tend a fire."

He rested his head in the loam. "No need to keep watch tonight. The aspen will alert me if something approaches. We will reach the lake by noon the day after tomorrow."

"How do you know that?"

"The aspens told me."

I unrolled my blanket. "That sounds like the perfect amount of time to tell me more about the city."

The leaves crunched as he pressed deeper into the loam. "You can read to your heart's content at the Archives."

I snuggled into my blanket. Somewhere nearby, Brother huffed and shifted his hooves. I hummed to him, then pulled my hat over my ears and eyes. "But maybe if I know something interesting about your time in the city, I can be more convincing when I have to explain why you aren't like the stories."

"Tell them a Harmonizer saved this aspen grove."

"Some group of humans a day and a half from here won't care about that."

"Exactly. You're the storyteller. Make them care."

I groaned. "Fine." I pulled up my blanket. If my family were here, Octavia would tell me to stop pestering him, but a Harmonizer who lived for so long, he had to have some great stories. Something stopped him from sharing even though I'd told him my story.

The leaves crumbled and crunched again. "Rowan?" He barely whispered it.

"Hmm?"

"I'm not good at—I don't know how to explain my memories. They aren't stories—to me. They aren't happy, either.

I'm not a storyteller. I don't know how to make them mean something."

I raised my head and twisted to look at him, but he still stared at the canopy, his eyes bright. "Maybe that's why I'm here."

He sighed. The glow of his eyes matched the moonlight sliding off the aspen bark. "I want to be forgotten, by all except for a few."

"I'll remember you."

"I know."

✦✦✦✦✦   ✦✦✦✦✦

The next morning, Eduardo quickened our pace, so I rode Brother as we left the woods behind for a meadow, then up the next hill, draped in a younger forest, most of the trees only a few decades old. Switchback trails cut into the hill, wide enough for two carts.

On the other side of the hills, we hurried into the valley, following dry creek beds until we came to a stream for Brother to drink from. My family summered in this valley, so I told Eduardo stories of the deer in the wildflowers and the black bears coming from the real mountains to the west. Once, Octavia had chased off a bear because the people who came before us hadn't buried their food waste, and it became a story my family laughed about every year.

We made good distance in the valley, even though the wind cut through the new growth trees. I walked alongside Brother so he blocked some of the wind, but Eduardo didn't seem to mind. He just took off his coat, so it stopped tangling around his legs.

Other nomadic communities passed through this valley, and a few farms dotted the meadows or clearings near the stream. Usually, they recognized Eduardo as soulkind and listened as we explained the city had expanded into the hills, but with a day's walk between them and that new expansion, most said thank you and avoided meeting our eyes. But it wasn't at all like the Riverroaders. I had expected more people like Brand or my Granmum, but most folks didn't hassle us, and some even smiled and invited us for a drink or some food.

We ate lunch with a group of hunters on a rise, watching an elk herd pass below and stayed the night in a hut at the base of the foothills. A few stone shelters had been built into the hillside long ago, and a large family had moved in to map the woods. They'd come over the pass to document the ecosystem and track its recovery. They asked Eduardo all kinds of questions about what he could sense of water pollution from mining run-off.

The next morning, they gave us the most direct route to the Archivists, and Eduardo promised to come back and help with the mapping if he could.

According to them, the Archivists managed a similar project, trying to restore the biome around a mine. Following the mining roads to the quarry was the fastest way to reach them from this direction.

Asphalt cut into the hillside, still young enough it had only begun to shimmy apart and crack. Eduardo pulled on his boots, and we took the road to the top of the hill.

The lake spread out below us, glinting in the overcast sun, except it didn't look like the ponds or pools my family camped beside. Rather than sloping to the water, the rocky sides looked like a big shovel had cut into the hill and levered out the middle. Trees and other foliage grew on top, but the sides stretched blank and rocky except for water lines. The water turned cloudy and red around the edges.

Eduardo shaded his eyes. "Ah, it's not a lake. No wonder it felt strange."

"That's a lot of water."

"That's the mine, filled up." He pointed at the rocky sides. "Coal or maybe mineral."

Brother left us to graze at the top of the hill as we passed through a narrow gorge, the only way down to the water. Other paths had been blocked with rubble or trees. As we struggled over the splintering limestone—at least, I struggled; Eduardo remained sure-footed—the gorge opened onto a stone platform with crumbling, lichen-spotted equipment. Some old flood had wedged a tree trunk between the two walls, and Eduardo ducked under it while I climbed on top and perched there.

Eduardo slapped a hand over his shoulder as if swatting a mosquito, almost bumping his head. "Did you feel that?"

I dangled my feet over the wind-smoothed trunk. "Huh?" The lake looked bigger from this angle than at the top. The water spread so dark it became a cloudy night sky. The occasional breeze blew the water's coolness over my skin, and I shivered. A metallic stink made me pull my scarf over my nose, but the breeze cleared away the smell.

We scuttled off the rocks and onto the platform. Other than the rusted equipment, no entrance or sign of a community broke up the rock and water.

Eduardo pressed his palm to the rock. "There's a community here, underground."

As if someone had heard him, a guttural *whoosh* sounded at the edge of the platform. A waterfall poured from a rock-hewn chute, thundering into the lake below. Mist swirled, catching on the rusting equipment.

A sound rose above the waterfall, like the wind in the trees, then dipped to a whirring like summer cicadas hidden in the canopy.

Eduardo lunged for me. "Rowan!" He dragged me behind him even though I was bigger than him. He kept a hold of my coat as if someone might try to rip me away.

"What?" My voice cracked. Nothing joined us on the platform.

"That was my language." He breathed hard through clenched teeth. "They knew my name. In my language. Nobody knows—"

"Apologies." A figure flickered in the mist above the waterfall, except they only appeared from the waist-up, as if floating.

Eduardo shoved me back, keeping his other hand raised as if he might grab at the mist. "Stay away."

"I am a projection on the mist. I cannot hurt you."

"Who are you?"

"We are an Archivist community." The wind blew away some of the waterfall mist, and the projection shimmered before stabilizing. The speaker seemed to be an older person with copper-brown skin, their black hair drawn up into a braid woven with red thread. "You're in our databases, and we greet those we know in their language. I apologize for the distress this has caused you. I will make note of it in your file. Would you like to come in?"

I tapped Eduardo's hand, and he loosened his grip but still angled himself in front of me. I leaned around him. "Yes, we want to come in! Thank you."

Eduardo frowned but nodded.

"The door is behind you." The projection sputtered away.

Eduardo twisted around, forcing me back. "Wait, all right? I need to be sure."

I sighed but nodded. He finally let go of my coat.

A rock slab we'd climbed over when coming through the gorge groaned and creaked upward, smaller bits and pieces of debris skittering aside. It rose on a cylinder set in a platform, making some sort of lift.

The person from the projection stepped off. "I'm she-Cara." She dusted off her red tunic, the edges embroidered with flowers. "Welcome to the Archives, Erhent."

I looked over at Eduardo—or was it Erhent? Had I heard that right? She couldn't have called him Erhent.

He frowned, but he finally lowered his outstretched hand. "It's Eduardo. You can call me he-Eduardo."

She bowed her head. "Apologies, again. I'll make note of that in your file, as well."

I waved. "I'm Rowan." If she had a whole file on him, then she had definitely called him Erhent. She must have. But Erhent had to be long dead.

Cara motioned us toward the rock-topped lift. "Well, welcome to the Archives! I can answer any questions you might have and teach you how to use the libraries."

The word "libraries" made my heart race. I hadn't been in a true library before, just the homemade collections of friends we passed on the road.

I stepped forward, but Eduardo touched my arm.

"How did you know my name? You said I was in your system."

"You have a hundred-and-fifty-year-old microchip in your left shoulder."

He looked over his shoulder as if he expected something to be growing out of his skin. "I do?"

"Shockingly, our perimeter system scanned it." She pointed at the tree trunk we'd passed when leaving the gorge. "You are in our archives, of course. We have many stories of humankind and soulkind working together, including ones about you. Under many names, though I'll note your preference for Eduardo."

I took a breath. *Under many names.* She must know part of his story, or I could find it somewhere inside. He couldn't actually be Erhent, could he? Those stories were centuries old, just legends. "So, you also go by—"

"That was long ago." He guided me toward the elevator. "We aren't here to use your databases, actually. We would like to have a warning broadcast, if you are willing."

I stepped into the elevator. Some sort of bioluminescent lichen or moss lined the walls. "I'd like to use the databases—if that's okay." And see if I could find proof about Eduardo. If *the* Erhent had just come across my family in the woods, now that would be a story.

Eduardo bumped my shoulder. "I know you do. There's time."

Cara heaved the sliding door shut. "Yes, time for all that, but first, let me welcome you properly with some food and a hot drink. It's chilly out there. How long have you two been traveling?"

"Just a few days," I said, "but it feels longer."

The elevator opened onto a stone-hewn tunnel propped with carved beams. Motion-activated lights lined the hallway. "This is our back door. Most of our visitors come from the north, but you must have come from near the city if you've been traveling a few days."

"That's what we came to talk to you about," I said. "The city is expanding. We're trying to warn any communities in its path."

"Ah." Cara looked back at Eduardo as if she knew something about him. "That's why you're traveling together."

"He saved my family," I said. "So I wanted to help."

Cara half-smiled. "He always does."

The hall ended in a door that looked like it came from another era, with a large wheel in the middle. Left ajar, Cara swung it open.

The next room spread so much bigger than our winter cave. I hadn't been in a room so big since I left the city years ago. A mix of ceiling shafts letting watery light waver onto tables, rechargeable lanterns, hand-crank flashlights, and bioluminescent plants lit the room. Tables clustered around tall lights operated by foot pedals, and readers pumped the pedals while they read or talked. At least twenty-five people worked at the long, wooden tables, with other lights roaming the book stacks lining the walls.

I stumbled forward. "Wow."

Cara was saying something about this just being one of the reference rooms—easier to control the temperature below ground—but that our rooms would be above ground, with windows.

I walked to the first bookcase. Most of the titles mentioned African myths and stories by different authors. Some of the books looked so brittle and yellowed I would be afraid to touch them. On the top shelf, the hardcovers looked identical, like they came from a different era, how Uncle Miguel described everything as mass-produced, not the mismatched, patched books I read.

Something Cara said pulled me into focus, and I glanced over my shoulder.

"I study war in the twenty-first century and—nobody knows—I don't think many know you're still alive. If we hadn't scanned you—"

"I prefer to keep it that way." Eduardo clasped his hands behind his back. "I'm not needed. Not like that—that time is long gone."

"Of course," Cara said. "If you... if you want to talk. I wasn't alive then, but I can listen."

Eduardo said thank you as I walked over, scuffing my feet since I already felt bad for listening. Even though Cara stood a head taller than him with enough wrinkles to be an elder, she seemed to have shrunk beside him.

"Why are there so many copies of the same book? That seems wasteful."

Cara clasped her hands. "You're right, it is. But it serves a purpose, here. One of the things Archivists study are the stories we tell ourselves about how we live. We all have stories we like to tell people about how we met, or about our favorite memories or places—isn't that right?"

I nodded.

She motioned at the bookshelves. "Well, what we look at is how the big stories we used to tell about humankind—how we came to be, why we built cities—how those stories are written and recorded over generations. Which ones are the most printed, the subtle changes in retellings, those kinds of things."

"What do you learn from that?"

Cara walked along a path lit by bioluminescent honey fungi clustered on either side. "That some parts of humanity loved to claim one version of a story was the truth and toss aside all the others. We don't want to make that mistake again."

As much as I could've dedicated hours to just reading the titles before even cracking a spine, Cara said she'd show me around later. The reference room exited onto a ramp that steadily rose, and Cara explained mine carts used to be dragged up this slope, though they had to modify it for human use. "We store many of the books and all our databases below ground as it's easier to control the temperature, but we do our living in the sunlight."

The shaft opened into a glass dome tall enough to curve over treetops. After the coolness underground, the dome's warmth made me unbutton my coat. A copse of alder, hawthorn, and birch greeted us, with rows of apple, cherry, and peach trees beyond. Among the trees, the ground exploded with life, even in the early winter. Small gardens in raised boxes, trickles of water washing beside the mossy footpaths, robins chirping in the trees, even a fox passed through a small meadow—I'd seen spaces like this when walking, but not so condensed. A warm springtime scent, like when the snowmelt streams came down the hills, greened the air.

Eduardo exhaled. "So much life in this dead space."

Cara passed into the small grove, trailing her hands over the trunks. "Slowly, the land is changing. We work to remove the pollution from the soil. All our water comes from the lake as we draw out the poison. We make enough compost to spread among the returning plants outside. The water gives us hydropower and the domes collect sunlight."

"Domes?" I asked. "There's more of these?"

"Two more, yes." She gathered a handful of cherries, offering them to me. I popped one into my mouth, sweet and tart, but the taste pulled me away from winter.

"Are you fully self-sufficient?" Eduardo asked.

"Only in the past fifty years, but it depends on how many visitors we have. We don't turn anyone away from our archives."

She led us to the center of the dome, where a clover field stretched, broken up by small streams. Pines shaded the edges. Someone had left a thermos and small box that unfolded into a tray of dried fruit, dried fish, cheese, fresh apples, and herbs to steep.

We settled on the clover. Eduardo sprawled on his back, his hands behind his head.

Cara asked what we would like to drink, and she steeped rosemary and lemongrass tea for me and chicory coffee for Eduardo. "So, you want to send a message." Cara poured our drinks into heavy ceramic mugs.

I spread soft cheese onto a piece of fish. "A warning. The city is expanding and nobody knows. Messengers from the city just came to where my family was wintering and said they would take half of us."

Cara raised her eyebrows. "Take?"

Eduardo hummed. "To balance. But Rowan's family was in balance. I could see that."

"How far is the city expanding?"

"Two day's ride." I pulled the map from my pack and spread it on the clover. I marked the hills where we wintered, never moving closer to the city for just this reason. "The city also built a dam here." I tapped where the river turned back toward the city as it followed the hills.

"A dam, really? For hydro-electric?"

Eduardo rolled on his side and propped his head in his hand. "Eventually, would be my guess. But for now, it seemed to be—a disruption." He frowned as he sipped his chicory coffee. "I couldn't risk approaching."

"I see. Would you be willing to tell your story to a council? We will broadcast your message, of course—anyone can use our equipment—but it sounds as if we should be prepared for what the city is doing."

"That's why we're here," I said. Apparently, I wouldn't have to convince them to listen to us or that Eduardo wasn't a threat. What made the Archivists different from the Riverroaders? Not all of them had mistrusted us, but Eduardo had caused a certain wariness, just like with my family. Maybe it was because Cara recognized him. That might be important to telling this story later, but he clearly didn't want me to ask.

Cara stood and brushed herself off. "I'll gather a council to meet after you've eaten and washed. Rest here, remember the sunlight, and I'll be back soon."

Eduardo said his thanks, then lounged on his back. He let out a long sigh.

I bit into a fresh apple. "That was easy."

"We haven't met the council yet, but yes. I trusted the Archivists to understand. All this has happened before." He shielded his eyes with his arm, but his other hand pressed into the clover, his fingers worked into the soil.

"Is everything happy here?"

"Hmm?"

"You're listening, aren't you? When you do that thing with your hand."

He chuckled. "Clever, kid. Everything wishes there was no need for the domes." He pointed behind us. "But everything hopes in a thousand years, the domes won't be necessary. Everything is working for the next millennium."

I popped a cherry into my mouth, then spit out the pit. "Sooo, I should still call you Eduardo?"

He sighed so deeply I felt like a little kid. "Yes, Rowan."

"But are you?"

He scratched at his shoulder. "The only thing that remembers Erhent is this fucking chip I forgot to cut out two centuries ago."

I winced, but I couldn't stop the smile. I hid my face by turning to watch the clouds. Erhent, a legend so fantastic stories of him entertained children too rowdy for sleep. He'd been a great warrior fighting for justice or he'd outsmarted the rich to help save forests and deserts and rivers from being polluted. And he was sitting right here, beside me. But why wouldn't he use his name? Even Brand couldn't have been scared of Erhent.

He clasped his hands over his stomach and sighed, seeming to sink into the clover. "It's just been a very long time since someone knew my name."

I glanced at him, still smiling, and he rolled his eyes.

"Well, not that long, it seems," he said. "You obviously recognize it."

"My favorite story is how you destroyed that river dam out West by convincing the greedy miners that there was gold inside it."

He sat up to sip his coffee. "That's not what happened. People died. My friends died."

I ran my fingers through the clover, much too green for this time of year. The story left out that part. Maybe the storytellers didn't want to scare the children or maybe those deaths had been forgotten.

Now, I understand his response a little better. Becoming Erhent again hid away all that pain that he still hadn't fully recovered from, perhaps never would. He had to be something else when he used that name—never tired, never scared, always ready for the next struggle.

"Was it worth it?" I asked. "The story says the canyon was so beautiful people cried to see it again."

He nodded. "The land had to be given back."

We settled into silence as I ate, and Eduardo sipped a second cup of chicory coffee. A few minutes later, Cara returned and led us back into the caves to the guest bath and communal closet. She said to take our time, as the council wouldn't convene for another hour.

The warm bath was a nice change from the stream I'd washed in yesterday, and I changed out my worn undershirt and socks for clean ones. Eduardo exchanged all his clothes, which hadn't held together very well with the riding and walking—except for his coat. He used the offered needle and thread to add two more patches along the shoulder seam where Brand had grabbed him.

The council took place in one of the dining halls, a long wooden structure built into the cliff that supported one side of the second dome, which contained most of the human spaces. Cara and six others joined us, including they-Reese, who was about my age. They brought me a plate of their favorite foods. It'd been ages since I'd eaten pasta, and Reese got me seconds.

Eduardo explained that the city was expanding with disregard to the needs of the rest of the living world, then I told the story of how Eduardo helped my family and added in the new piece about the Riverroaders, the dam, and how some of their kayakers would spread the warning along the tributaries.

I ended with the broadcast request. "The Riverroaders suggested we find you because you could broadcast a warning to any who want to leave. I know the smaller groups won't all have radios—my family doesn't—but hopefully some of the larger communities will hear it."

Ze-Richel shifted on the bench seat, rubbing zir lower back. I'd gathered ze was eight months pregnant from the care of the other council members, like Reese who had asked if ze needed any more food or fruit juice. "Forgive me for this intrusion into your past, Eduardo, but we know who you are. We are inclined to take anything that worries you very seriously. Have you just come from Haven City? Some Archivists work in the city libraries, but they haven't given any cause for concern."

I glanced at Reese, but they shrugged. At least I wasn't the only one who hadn't known Eduardo's past as Erhent. Maybe he'd explain some things.

He shifted back from the table. "I didn't come here to be treated like a war hero. I want to use your broadcast equipment, that's all."

Reese leaned their elbows on the table. "I don't think of you as a war hero. I like the city, but I like all the rocks and trees and hills around it, too. Why can't things stay the way they are?"

Eduardo squeezed his eyes shut and massaged his forehead. "You're right, Reese. Rowan, can I see your map?"

I spread the map on the table.

"I've lived in the city for the past decade because I'd seen other cities transform into something harmonious with the rest of the living world. For a few years, it seemed all right. The city was vibrant and content, and for the most part, the Harmonizers lived peacefully, but many of them couldn't let go of the idea that they were meant to harness humanity for something greater. That old rhetoric is always appealing to some, particularly certain elders."

"Were they willing to listen to you?" Cara asked.

Eduardo ducked his head. "I didn't say anything. I was just another soulkind elder come to the easy city. I wanted to see if the old lines were true, if city-living with the Harmonizers was more sustainable. I always thought we were needed out here." He spread his hand over the map. "So many places are broken or sick or choking, and we can spend the decades to bring those places back into balance."

I hadn't realized he'd been in the city for all those years. We could have been there at the same time, if my memories were accurate. Now that would be a story, if we'd crossed paths in the city, only to travel together years later.

He-Ash, an elder, tapped his knuckles against the table. "Two centuries ago, our earliest buildings were based off that idea—to bring balance and healing, no matter how long it took."

"Plant sequoias," Reese said, and the others nodded as if it were some sort of saying.

Eduardo picked at his fingernails. "I first thought something might be wrong when the green spaces in the city started being replaced with more buildings. The Harmonizers claimed climate refugees had come and the city needed more space, but I'd only seen Harmonizers bringing in more humans. After a few years, the city did feel crowded, so the Harmonizers raised the prices."

"Prices?" I asked. "What do you mean?"

Cara watched Eduardo for a moment, then said, "Anything living in the city pays for it through calories, energy, taken by the Harmonizers."

"Oh." That explained Brand's fear, my Granmum's worry. Back then, I'd never paid with my body, rarely paid for anything, let alone with myself. The stories made what the Harmonizers did sound like reciprocity or give-and-take, not a demand for payment.

"So the city expands," Ash said. "Calls it harmonizing or balancing, and, what? Why do the Harmonizers of the city want to gather more humans?"

Eduardo traced a finger from where I'd roughed out a blob-shaped city to the X of the cave entrance. "Judging from how far they came after Rowan's family, I think they are enjoying their lifestyle and want it to grow bigger, better."

"Can you be sure?" Richel asked.

Eduardo shook his head. "I set out to warn the communities because I wanted them to have a choice, not be surprised like Rowan's family or the Riverroaders at the dam. I have to balance for not speaking up before it was too late."

Ash took out a short length of rope and looped a knot, then undid it. "A dam. We know better than that. Why would the Harmonizers purposefully unbalance the area?"

Eduardo worried at a hangnail until it spotted blood. "You need to forget about the Harmonizers as believing in balance. Those were just stories meant to control desperate people."

"Scholars have studied that possibility, yes," Cara said.

Ash untangled his length of rope. "Yet many of us have learned from your way of listening and seeing the world."

"And I've learned from you." Eduardo hid his hands under the table. "You and the Riverroaders and Rowan's family are all trying to live in harmony. No one has the only answer, but you all have pieces of it, and so do I."

"So," Reese said, "you think the city forgot that."

"This city, yes."

Richel rested a hand on xir belly. "Do you have a proposal for a response? You have your message to share, but is there something you believe we should be doing?"

Cara nodded. "Most likely, the expansion won't impact us directly, but the overall impact on the environment will reach us."

"Contact the Archivists in the city," Eduardo said. "See if they can attend any city council meetings or if humans have been barred from attending. It would at least be helpful to know what stories the Harmonizers are telling the people."

Ash pocketed his rope. "Thank you, Eduardo and Rowan, for coming to tell us. If you'd like to record your message now, I can show you how to use the radio equipment."

Reese stood. "I'll come, too!" They hurried to clear the plates, running from the table to the dirty dishes cart.

❦

Ash led us into the underground portion to a room filled with different screens and switchboards. Eduardo planned to record a short message tonight, then we would both record something longer tomorrow that would play on loop on a separate channel. I wasn't quite sure what Ash meant, but Eduardo seemed to think that would be the best path.

While he recorded with Ash, Reese taught me how to use the Archivist's databases. They'd come to the Archivists to research a certain compost recipe for their family's farm. The topsoil had been depleted, so they were searching for the best way to replenish the area while, if possible, supporting human agriculture.

Reese could breeze through the databases, but I had to write down which buttons to click. Each search word collected hundreds of responses.

"Is there something you want to look up?" Reese asked.

My fingers itched to search *Erhent*, but I couldn't do that in front of Reese, and it seemed like Eduardo would be upset if I dug into his past. Even though I had told him all I knew about my story, I couldn't expect him to share the same.

As I stumbled for a different search term, I overheard Ash's conversation with Eduardo.

"Levels looked fine this time," Ash said. "But are you sure you don't want to use a different name?"

"It's too dangerous."

"Yes, but it could motivate—"

"I don't want to be responsible for that kind of motivation. Not again."

Reese raised their eyebrows. "That's the second time the elders have talked like that. Do you know who he is?"

"I just found out this morning because Cara recognized him. I don't think Eduardo would want me to say." Back then, part of me thought Ash was right. If a warning from *the* Erhent said the city was in the wrong, wouldn't that be a good thing?

Reese shrugged. "Fair enough. What type of storyteller do you want to be?" They launched into an explanation of where to find the physical books, especially the novels and folklore collections.

By then, Eduardo had finished, and we all listened to the short message broadcasting every hour: "This is the Harmonizer Eduardo. The city limits are expanding to the Hawk Hills and the Riverbed Range. As of now, north of the river is still outside of city limits. The Archivists are open to anyone in need of help."

"We always monitor the radio," Ash said. "If any responses come in, we'll be sure to let you know."

CHAPTER FIVE

T he next morning, there was a response all right. Cara found us in the dining hall. Reese had just joined us and was chattering about showing us around the three domes.

Cara slid onto the bench beside them. She leaned over the table, glancing at the door she'd just come through. "City emissaries are here."

Eduardo half-stood, scanning the room. "Then it's time for us to leave."

"I told them you already did," Cara said. "They asked for you but didn't seem bothered you had supposedly left. There's other soulkind staying with us—you shouldn't stand out."

"That seems fast," Reese said. "They must have already been in the valley."

"Or traveling by vehicle," I said.

Eduardo flipped up his hood. He took a knit cap from his pocket and handed it to me. "Did they say anything else?"

"Nothing to alarm us," Cara said. "If that's what you're asking. They're meeting with some different councils, then they asked to speak to the people." She reached across the table. "I don't think you or Rowan are in danger, Eduardo. I just didn't want you to be surprised."

"I've brought dangerous guests to your door," Eduardo said.

Cara tossed her long braid over her shoulder. "We live in harmony here, working to restore this place. We have nothing to fear from Harmonizers—you or any others."

I tucked my hair into the knit cap. "Can we go listen to them?"

Eduardo stiffened so fast I thought his joints would groan. "Absolutely not. You saw what they did."

"That's why I want to go. I want to see what these emissaries are like."

He straddled the bench to face me. "Rowan, we've done our duty. The message has gone out. It's time for you to go back to your family."

Part of me knew he was right. My family would be a few days west of here, waiting in the valley where the river came down from the mountain pass, but the storyteller I wanted to be whispered no, what kind of story was this? I'd never know if our warning had been heard, if we'd done any good. And I'd certainly never see the city, even though I was supposed to go in the spring. Uncle Miguel would never take me anywhere near the limits after all this. I'd never return to the cave or learn if the orchard survived. My family would be afraid that the city might swoop in again, like an eagle after a pup.

I braced against the table edge. "I don't think I'm ready to leave yet. I want to see the Archives, and I want to record a longer warning message to send, so people who hear it understand what's going on."

Eduardo looked away, his jaw twitching. "You don't understand."

He was right, I didn't understand. I hadn't been fed on before, or even sat with the stories of his past, what he'd lived through and the pain he'd watched those he loved endure. Sometimes, I'm shocked he didn't drag me back to my family. If the roles had been reversed, I would have insisted, but in his wisdom, he knew better than to force me, even if it made him afraid.

"Rowan's safe here if you feel the need to leave, Eduardo," Cara said. "We haven't had that type of violence visited here in decades."

Eduardo scrubbed a hand down his face. "Fine, fine. Do you have masks—for when someone isn't feeling well?"

The city emissaries offered to answer questions and talk with the people over lunchtime. We joined a crowd of maybe fifty people in the second dome, beneath a large oak tree. Stone slabs made benches around a stump-turned-table, where a mix of fresh fruit and vegetables and dried fish waited alongside pitchers of cold herbal tea. Even in winter, the domes kept the air warm enough that chilled tea sounded delightful.

Some folks took the benches, including the Harmonizers, while others sat in the sun or against the tree. Eduardo guided me to the left, not directly in the Harmonizers' sight, and we sat in the grass. Reese dropped down beside me.

Cara motioned to the food and drinks. "Please, enjoy yourself. We're happy to talk more about what it means to live here." She sat next to the Harmonizers.

They looked like the ones who had come to my family, dressed in dark city clothes, crisp and unpatched. Even their shoes were clean. Their faces didn't look familiar, but like the others, these Harmonizers stood well over six feet tall with frost-pale skin. The tallest and sparest two stayed quiet except to agree with the third one. They had long, white hair braided down their backs, and their eyes shone in the afternoon light.

The third one seemed the most like what I imagined an emissary to be. He talked, joked, and asked questions. The shortest of the three, he didn't have the same spare build, but reminded me of a black bear, powerful with big shoulders. Instead of the long white hair, he'd cut his hair short, curling around his ears, which emphasized the smile he offered too often. He'd been the only one to introduce himself, shaking hands: Johnny.

Johnny turned to Cara as if speaking privately, but his voice pitched loud enough for everyone to hear. "All of this is thoughtfully designed and doing the work of balancing the harm that's come before. But in the city, you don't have to worry about that." He tapped his chest. "My kind take care of that, and you're free to study or create or even just relax. Harmony is for you—you don't have to try to find it anymore, like this never-ending attempt you are making here."

Eduardo dug his fingers into the grass. He whispered, "Liar."

One of the Archivists, he-Ty, drifted forward and braked his chair beside the stump table. He poured a glass of tea, then offered one to Cara. "I don't think any of us are bothered by the trying, if that's what you're asking. I'm not, at least. It's part of how I connect and feel at home with the rest of the world."

Johnny stood to pour himself a glass but kept standing, as if he'd stepped onto a stage. "Once we expand into the valley, we'll be neighbors—"

"The valley?" A voice cracked. Judging from the thick travel clothes, the person was a newcomer to the Archives, like us. "Why—why the valley?"

Johnny's smile turned into something more like a smirk. "The valley isn't reaching the fullest potential possible, so we want to help it along."

I glanced at Eduardo, his glaring visible even with the cloth mask covering his mouth and nose. The city would be expanding farther than we'd imagined—hundreds of miles. My family still wouldn't be safe, then. We'd have to cross the hills to the north beyond the Archives or take the pass to the west. We didn't know the land over there, though we'd met travelers from those places. But most of the valley folk weren't nomads. Where could they go after years or decades of preparing the soil and learning the seasons, the weather, the migration patterns?

Eduardo leaned over and whispered, "Tell Reese to ask how a valley can have potential."

I passed it along to Reese, who raised their hand. "Valleys don't have potential. They just are."

Johnny wagged a finger at them. "Smart kid. See, we need thinkers like you working at the city. Now, you and I, we're part of nature, too—am I right?"

Reese and some others nodded.

"So that means our survival and growth is important to the environment, too, just like it takes many species to create a healthy forest. You still following?"

More nods.

"That's what we're going to use the valley for. Our mutual growth. As the city expands, more humans will come from places where the land hasn't recovered enough to support them. That is why we're expanding, to help us *all* recover." He motioned to the domes. "You're practicing these principles on a smaller scale. We're just expanding that scale, for the mutual benefit of all living beings."

The person who asked about the valley raised their hand slightly. "Will those of us who—who don't want to be in the city limits. Will we be given notice of when to leave? The radio announcement said—"

Johnny huffed. "Oh, please, ignore that other Harmonizer. I came here hoping to talk to him for just that reason. He's been spreading lies all through this territory. There's nothing for the valley dwellers to fear. Of course you will have plenty of time to leave if you don't wish to join the city." He walked closer to the person, who sat in the grass a few yards from us. "But please, at least hear us out when we come to your door. Our expansion into the valley is for the good of everyone. You need not fear going hungry or thirsty again."

The questioner took a deep breath and looked up at Johnny. "I don't fear that now."

Johnny flashed ice-white teeth. "Then you are ready for the solidarity of the city."

Eduardo leaned back on his hands, his fingers digging even deeper into the dirt as if steadying himself. "What happens when a human enters the city for the first time?"

"Oh, this old chestnut." Johnny brushed off his hands. "We take your name, age, any other important information, then we make an exchange of energy."

Several people looked away or grimaced. I glanced at Reese, but they shrugged a shoulder.

Johnny clapped his hands together. "Come now. You all give your blood, sweat, and tears to this land. You've broken bones, sickened, frozen, ached, and bled for this place. There's no difference from that feeling and what you exchange with us. We are *all* part of this environment. The city's expansion is for us *all* to thrive. How else can we build a healthy, harmonizing community?"

The way Johnny described it seemed at odds with the fear my family had shown when the Harmonizers arrived, or the fear that Brand placed on Eduardo being near me. Johnny's ideas made sense with what I'd been taught about how to live. That's why my family still killed for meat—an exchange—though not all those who wintered with us or traveled with us did so.

The group broke up after Johnny's explanation, but about half stayed to talk and ask more questions about the city. Eduardo and I left with Reese, hurrying out of the dome back down to the libraries.

"That was—strange," Reese said. "I don't think I see how this so-called exchange is the same as working in a garden."

"Because it's not," Eduardo said. He led us into a reference room, finding an alcove of empty chairs, far from the doors. We'd be just shadows to anyone walking through. He sank into a chair and rested his head in his hands. "It's not even how we are—how our bodies work."

I dragged a chair closer to his and waited for him to raise his head. If I hadn't seen how the soulkind treated my family, I would have asked to go back to the city with Johnny. I would have believed him, even if the whole exchange thing sounded funny. I wanted to live as lightly on the land as possible and help others do that. If that was the promise of the city, I would have made that pact.

Eduardo let out a long breath. "Do you know when they are leaving, Reese?"

"Later today, I think. Unless they change their minds."

Eduardo tugged off his mask and tucked it in his pocket. "All right, then. Tomorrow, if Cara and the council believe it's safe, I'll help record a new message, then Rowan and I will leave." He rubbed his hands together hard enough his knuckles cracked. "If it's safe—I don't know."

Reese stood. "I'll check in with Cara once they're gone, but I don't think you need to be so worried. People will do what they want. If they want to go to the city, they'll listen to Johnny." They headed off with a wave.

"I think you're right," I said to Eduardo. "I would have trusted Johnny if I hadn't seen how they tried to take my family. We need to make sure people hear another story."

Asphalt sucking me down woke me, gasping and kicking at my blankets. I'd dreamed of the city before, but not for years. I wiped sweat off my face with the blanket. I didn't usually worry about the city. It was one way to live, a choice I'd decided to leave behind. Now, it was coming for the places I loved and—the winter cave would be gone. The apple orchard would never have the chance to regrow. The deer that passed by on the misty mornings as the snow melted—all of it would soon be gone.

As my breathing calmed, a creaking-wheeze came from the other side of the door. I crouched to peer under the bottom crack. A cone of light illuminated boots.

I stood and eased open the door.

Eduardo read in a rocking chair, each rock pushing a pedal to power a reading lamp. "Did I wake you?" He marked his spot with his thumb.

"No, I—what are you doing here?"

"Just reading." He held up a ragged book titled *Cien años de soledad*. "I don't sleep as much as you think I do."

I looked down the dark hall. "Do you think we're not safe here?"

"No, no. Not at all. Don't worry yourself."

Without his rocking, the light flickered out.

"Then why are you outside the room?"

The light whirred as he operated the foot pedal. "I thought your family usually slept in the same room, and that maybe you hadn't slept by yourself since the time before you were safe."

I sat on the floor, my back to the wall. "I had a nightmare. I was in the city again, and the road was sucking me down, like a muddy river bottom. I couldn't crawl free."

"Well, tomorrow we'll record one more message, then leave to find your family. You will all go far beyond whatever new limits the city sets."

I drew up my knees and hugged them. That wasn't what made me still feel clammy. The city didn't always strike fear. Some chose to live there because they thought it was the best way to live in relationship with the rest of the world. Some people found it easier, particularly when they were older, to live in the city. Others died on the road rather than live under the Harmonizers. I didn't remember much of the city except for being alone. But why had I been alone among so many people?

Eduardo stretched and stood. "Frowning isn't going to get you back to sleep. Let's explore."

I scrambled up. "Really?"

He tucked his book under his arm. "C'mon."

After listening to Johnny yesterday, Eduardo had insisted we stay in our rooms or in the shadowy corners of a reading room, which hadn't been so bad. I'd chosen a stack of books and huddled in a big chair with a solar-battery light, but Reese had said there were two other big libraries, plus the data centers.

According to Reese, nothing strange had happened with the soulkind. They'd said their piece, taken a tour, and left. Eduardo didn't seem satisfied, and their actions were a complete turnaround from how they acted with my family or with the Riverroaders. The Archivists represented a larger, more powerful group. To the Harmonizers, those kinds of politics or hierarchies weren't supposed to matter—balancing the harm to the living world is what counted. Maybe not to these city Harmonizers, though.

Even in the middle of the night, the Archives buzzed. People came and went, holding solar lights or crank lanterns. The motion-activated hall lights remained on more often than they blinked off. People carried steaming cups, and we stopped at a hot plate to pour ourselves mugs, rosemary and lemongrass tea for me and chicory coffee for Eduardo.

He blew on his cup. "All right, kid, where do you want to go?"

My nightmare had left me jittery, so we kept walking, exploring the different shafts. We found rooms that housed the energy storage, long spaces growing mushrooms under UV lights, floor-to-ceiling hydroponic systems. A technician told us that the lake water needed filtering, so the hydro system ran massive amounts of water through different filtration areas, including algae tanks, ponds, and hydroponics growing saplings to replant the hills. One of the large algae tanks had turned brown, and we watched two Archivists run contamination tests.

We followed the ramps toward the surface and found the main library. Closer to the surface, large shafts had been cut into the ceiling and one wall, and moonlight fractaled in blues and greens through stained glass. Big, wooden pillars rose to the ceiling, with bioluminescent fungi growing along the wood. Motion-activated lights also flicked on and off as people passed. In corners where the light couldn't reach, people used foot-pedal lights as they talked or read in cushion-strewn corners or in little alcoves made by the angle of couches and rocking chairs.

Beneath tables clustered under the biggest skylights, and people read, talked, and studied books by lamp light. Some had books stacked around them as they took notes on keyboards or rough sheets of paper. Others worked at tables along the walls, which had been smoothed enough they could be written on. One Archivist had a ladder leaned against the wall as they followed a mathematical trail up the stone.

But the best part was the bookcases. Twice my size, they towered like a forest, ringing the clearing in the middle. The walls of books muffled the echoes of the mining shaft. A pleasant mustiness, like dry leaves, spread through the underground space.

This space had the same cozy comfort as the winter cave, but so much bigger and with so many more people. Even at night, there must be more than a hundred people using the library. The other difference was how the Archivists treated the space. Maybe because I'd always lived nomadically, I didn't realize how decorative a place could be. Plants grew beside the windows or even in pots on the table. Many of the tables had etchings on the surface—vistas of the valley or pleasing patterns. Weavings covered the walls that hadn't been smoothed for writing, their scenes or colors only coming to light when somebody walked by. Even the ceiling dripped design. Wind chimes glinted in the light, sometimes tinkling at unfelt currents, and wire twisted into fantastic shapes twirled from hangers. My family had decorated some things, with carvings or different knitting or sewing patterns, but we couldn't keep many such things with us on the road. Even as a child, I had agreed with them, that the rest of the living world had plenty of beauty and that there was little need to capture it in art—why hang a weaving when a spider could make a more spectacular web? But to step into this space carved unasked from the mountainside and have it made so beautiful, so full of good, delightful things, it made me want to settle deep into a chair with a stack of books, submersed in comfort.

Even though I just wanted to get lost in the bookshelves, I had a feeling Eduardo was still a little too spooked to lose sight of me, so I settled for a research room, which was split between database terminals and stacks of reference books.

Eduardo leaned against the doorframe, one hand in his pocket. "Go on. Tell me what you find."

I tried out the terminals first. I'd used a computer before, but we usually didn't carry a tablet with us. These large screens were made from glass, the text fuzzy green against a black background. I skimmed the help module before I typed in Haven City.

As late night turned to early morning, the Archives quieted, and I passed hours going from the terminal to the reference books, looking up historical documents, maps, listening to oral stories, paging through a handbook of the flora and fauna of the area. Two hundred and fifty years ago it had been a mining town, then a lumber town, then a fracking boom city. The hills, caves, forests, and waterways had been decimated, even though the government back then claimed to be fighting climate change. The reference stacks collected heavy books of glossy pictures showing what the region used to look like, before lake waters flooded and receded, how the hills had been scooped away in the last attempts to find fuel.

I was searching for a book on the city's architecture when scuffling feet broke the quiet. Light flashed like a bulb burning out, then something heavy *thumped* the ground.

I ran out of the stacks and skidded around the final bookshelf.

The three Harmonizers filled the doorway. The two pale ones with the long blond braids bent over Eduardo, who had crumpled to the ground.

I sprinted toward him. Of course, it had all been too easy—Eduardo had known. I should have listened to him, but I'd trusted them to leave, taking them at that word. And now he was hurt.

Johnny raised his hands and stepped between us. "Now, now. He's fine. We just needed to balance him."

My hands clenched into fists. "Eduardo is in balance! That's all he does is bring balance to the places he stays." I followed Eduardo's warning and stayed a few steps out of reach.

Johnny smiled, showing too many teeth. "Oh, so *this* is Eduardo. Funny how he came back so soon. And that makes you his little friend. Rowan, isn't it?"

One of the others called to Johnny. "Take a look at this one."

He held up a finger. "Just one second, Rowan." He bent over Eduardo's still body and gripped his face, turning him toward the light.

I stomped forward a step. "Leave him alone!" I imagined crashing something over his head, but then what?

"Huh." Johnny clicked his tongue. "Look-y here. A real war hero."

"Should we take him with us?"

Johnny dropped Eduardo's head. "No, he'll follow us, I guarantee it. We've already taken him down once." He faced me and raised his hands. "See, he's fine, kiddo."

"What do you want with him?"

He crouched, hands braced on his knees. "Not with him. With you—to talk to you, invite you to see Haven City for yourself. It would be my honor to show you my city."

Behind him, the other two still hovered over Eduardo. His chest rose and fell. His fingers twitched.

I skirted sideways, but Johnny straightened, blocking my view. I only came to his chest. "If you love your city, why are you here?"

"I'm sharing the good news of the expansion. The land is healing, so it's time to grow together. You could be part of that, Rowan. We have the best storytellers, the best libraries, the best equipment." He motioned at the bookcases. "Imagine this but so much more, and not in a cave, but with big, open windows and all the light you could need."

"This is enough."

"But it doesn't have to be enough." Johnny nodded at the other two, and they returned to the hall, looking both ways. "Harmony doesn't mean we are all equal. Some are meant to work for the greater good." He reached for me, and I flinched back. "That other one, filling your head with nonsense." He smiled and shook his head. "Rowan, you have greatness in your bones. That greatness is waiting for you in the city. Just come for a visit. You can even bring him if you want." He returned to the entrance, stepping over Eduardo. "Careful, though, he's going to remember his hunger when he comes around."

Johnny flashed his teeth. "I'm sure I'll see you again." He vanished into the dark hallway.

I ran to Eduardo. "Wake up, wake up!" I touched his hand but jerked back. Human skin couldn't become so hot. Thin cracks spread from between his knuckles and along his wrist, almost like veins.

I shook him by his coat. "Erhent!"

He sucked in air, arching his back. He rolled onto his side, away from me. "Damn. That was my move. They used my move." He struggled onto his knees.

"Are you all right?" we both asked in unison.

Eduardo trembled. "I need to eat. Quickly."

I reached for his arm to shoulder him up, but he shrank back.

"I could burn you."

By the door, the Archivists kept tools to help get around, so I wheeled over a chair. Eduardo climbed into it.

"The filtration system." He gasped. "The broken tank."

Like when he'd fought the soulkind before, the skin around his hands appeared cracked and glowed white. I ran down the hallway, outpacing the motion lights. So late at night, we only passed one other person, a stranger, and I yelled for them to wake Cara, sound a warning, but before

I finished speaking, a low *blat blat* thrummed through the quiet hall.

I almost spilled Eduardo turning into the filtration room. He hauled himself into the low, long tank, stuffed with brown algae.

Steam *whooshed* from the tank, and the water level dropped. The brown algae vanished, and Eduardo's hand pressed against the glass as he held himself underwater. The light cracking and charring his skin receded.

The water cleared, and Eduardo burst through the surface. He shook the water from his hair. "Did they hurt you?"

"No, I—"

"I'm going to kill them." He swung out of the tank.

"I'm fine—"

He stalked into the hall. His soaking clothes dripped, but he shook himself again and steam ghosted off. Only a few damp footprints marked the floor.

"Eduardo, wait!" I ran after him.

Cara met us in the hallway. "What's going on?"

"Where are they?" he asked.

"The Harmonizers—"

"Tell me where they are!"

"They've already run off!" She clenched her fists. "We think they sneaked in a few hours ago. Destroyed our radio equipment and left."

"Why didn't you stop them?" Eduardo asked.

"We're a peaceful people, Eduardo. We can rebuild what they broke."

Eduardo made a sound in this throat. "Which exit?"

She pointed behind us.

He gripped my shoulders and drew me close so we were almost eye-to-eye. "Stay. Here."

"Eduardo, don't bring violence back to us," Cara said. "None were killed."

He padded down the hallway. "This time."

Cara stood by my side as Eduardo disappeared into the low light. "He'll be fine, Rowan. He knows what he's about."

I couldn't tell her about how they'd knocked him out with just a touch in case speaking it would make it happen again. He wanted to leave yesterday, and I should have listened. He knew better. I clasped my hands together, squeezing until my fingers cracked. *Please, please come back.*

CHAPTER SIX

For the next two days I read about the climate wars, how cities like Haven came into being, how humanity chose to survive and adapt. Each time Erhent's name came up, I scrolled past, turned the page. He didn't want me to know. Part of me hoped that if I left his story unread, then he'd have to come back and tell it to me.

All the books and articles sounded bleaker than how I'd learned it from Uncle Miguel, though he didn't specialize in the Post-Capitalist era of the Harmonizers. While several climate wars were ongoing at the time—over oil, water, and soil—the Harmonizers started one over land mass. They believed that half of the land mass should be set aside to replenish. If humans died or lost everything because of the move to "balance," then so be it. And like any war, many humans and nonhumans did die, but the Harmonizers were so deadly, able to kill or maim with a single touch, that they soon became the only threat. Some people agreed with their plan, as environmentalists had already proposed such theories. Now, something more-than-human had melted from the glaciers to enforce these ideas.

After a hundred years, climate disasters and the Harmonizers had broken apart the economic systems and dominant ways of thinking that had caused the climate to change. As humans focused on building local communities that could weather extreme events and wouldn't pollute or damage the rest of the living world enough to cause the Harmonizers to come and put them in "balance," the world I knew took shape.

Erhent's name threaded these histories. Without delving deeper, it seemed he'd fought against both the violence of the Harmonizers and the violence of the fossil fuel empires or the water barons. He'd saved communities during tornados or wildfires and helped them flee from Harmonizers or fossil fuel drillers come to take the land, just like the stories I'd listened to as a child had promised.

When my head ached from reading, I'd leave the domes and climb out of the quarry. Sometimes, Brother would meet me. I'd hoped he'd gone with Eduardo to help him, but he stayed close to the domes, grazing. Like Eduardo would, I'd stretch on the frozen ground, digging my fingers into the dirt. I'd close my eyes and press all my thoughts into the soil. He didn't want to be Erhent anymore, but I needed him to come back. Without him, I didn't know what to do except run away to my family, but there had to be more. I wasn't ready to give up.

And if Eduardo didn't come back, I would go searching for him, all the way to the city.

One evening a week later, a forager found a trail through undergrowth lush with winter greens uncatalogued before—holly, winterberry, violets, and fallen, decomposing trees thick with oyster mushrooms, brick caps, and chaga. A scout followed the trail until they spotted Eduardo sitting at the quarry's edge. Cara found me in the library and asked if I'd like to see him first.

I only paused to brew a thermos of chicory coffee. I didn't know what other gesture to make.

He dangled his feet over the rocky edge. His boots set beside him, and he clutched his coat in his lap, hiding his hands. His sleeves were rolled past the elbow, like he'd just come from fighting.

Below, the water turned deep and dark as a second night sky. Around us, what survived of the hills cut shadows along the horizon. My breath spiraled in the crisp, cold night, the air so clear the stars glittered and the moon's horns looked sharp enough to gore.

I waited a few yards back, scuffing my feet. Two heavy ceramic mugs clinked in my shaky hands. I'd imagined his return, running up to him and hugging him hard enough he would have to know how much I'd worried. I'd imagined him happy, relieved, not this brittleness that stole my breath like the icy wind.

He glanced over his shoulder. "I'm all right, Rowan."

I exhaled and hurried to him. "You were gone so long, Eduardo." I wanted to hug him, but he felt different, cold as the moonlight and sharp as the shale. Either he really needed a hug or that would only upset him.

He made a noise in his throat. "Oh, Eduardo. Still trying so hard." He raised his voice. "You should call me Erhent, now. I'm sure you've looked me up, with all those stories at your fingertips."

I sat beside him. "I didn't. You asked me not to." I unscrewed the thermos lid and poured him a mug. I offered him the handle.

He let out a breath, and his shoulders relaxed. His hand shook as he took the mug, careful our fingers didn't touch. His skin was red and chapped, but I knew not from the cold. "I should stop pretending. I'm not Eduardo—not just Eduardo." He cupped the mug in both hands, staring into

it. Steam swirled over his face. "How long was I gone?"
"A whole week."

"Was I?" He took a sip and his hands steadied. "Hmm,
a whole week. We don't have much time, then." He sat
straighter and shook his head, so his hair fell back. "Are
you ready to leave the Archivists? You need to be with
your family."

I fiddled with the thermos, breathing in the
sweet-smokey scent. While Erhent was gone, I'd talked
with Reese and Cara about where to go next. They would
repair their radio and had already rigged a system to pass
along the message on smaller, personal radios positioned
by scouts and foragers, but going back to my family felt
like a misstep, like choosing to take the same trail because
I knew every root and dip. Cara suggested we continue
north to a smaller city called Open Gates. No Harmonizers controlled this city, and humans worked together
with Harmonizers to help the city balance and heal. She
thought we could learn what a healthy city looked like in
order to help people understand why this expansion was
an imbalance. Hopefully, we could convince more people
not to simply shrug and say, leave it the Harmonizers.

"You wanted to leave before," I said. "I insisted we
didn't, then you got hurt. If you think it's time to go, I'll
trust you." I took a deep breath. "But I don't think the
story is over. The people in the valley—"

He set aside the mug. "The Archivists know what to
do. Our work is done. Except taking you to your family."

The words spun around my chest, and I shut my mouth
before I said something angry. Without the radio, we'd
warned just a handful of people. If the Harmonizers wanted
to keep us quiet enough to come to the Archive and break
their equipment, then it just meant this story was more important than I knew. I needed to keep telling it. I didn't want

to keep going for the adventure, but because I'd have to face the city someday. I couldn't keep running.

I poured myself a mug and clutched it to my chest for warmth. So close to the lake, the air felt crisp but heavy, like it might snow. Not clean, though, as a sour taste slicked my tongue. "Cara told me about another city called Open Gates. They need to be warned—the smaller radios can't reach them over the hills. I'm not afraid. I believe in our story. Breaking the radio is another part of it. I want to know where it all leads."

"Your story will not stop them." A bite edged his words, and I leaned back. He stood, glaring down at me. "If the Harmonizers want to expand the city, they will until they are satisfied." He pointed toward the shadowy hills. "They'll take all of it, especially if you care about it. You are safest with your family far away from here, and you can keep telling this story." He took a shaky breath. "Tell how you saved the old hero Erhent in an apple orchard. You can keep spreading this warning and hope the Harmonizers remember we don't have to take, we can heal."

I took a long sip of the chicory coffee, then slowly stood. His brittleness had cracked into a hurt and fear older than I could understand. Back then, I didn't know what to say to help. Even now, I struggle with those kinds of words.

I reached for his hand, but he stepped aside.

"What did I say—never touch a Harmonizer!"

I stayed still, my hand offered.

He paced back and forth, his feet bare. "You don't understand, Rowan. I took care of the Harmonizers. I put one in the aspen grove, and the other two under these hills. Once those places heal, they will have the strength to wake and walk again, hopefully understanding how to heal, not just take." His eyes were as bright as the moon glancing off the quarry lake. "When I found them, they threatened you. They threatened this place. They said how the city was going to spread and take this all away, just like the old days. That's what they want, to control everything, to control you."

"I'm not afraid."

He stomped his bare foot into the rock, cratering it. "You should be! I fought and fought and fought! And it was still destroyed. My homes were destroyed, the trees I loved destroyed, the beings and places I loved starving and flooding and ripped apart when there wasn't enough oil or water or soil. And I fought it so hard. I did everything, everything! And it's all gone!" His words echoed off the rock. He took a heaving breath. "I won't fight like that again. There's no reason to fight because they will just take it all away."

The stories I knew of Erhent, the rebel and hero, the glimpses from the database—I saw all the inspiring victories, the times he'd held back worse destruction or saved people. This place might not be the future he fought for, but it was still beautiful and thriving and alive, even if he forgot.

He limped toward me, leaving footprints that glistened wet with blood. Twice, he reached for my hand before I just did it for him. He dragged me into the tight, long hug meant to work through fear. "I would have been there, when—when you ran away from the city. I knew terrible things were happening, like what the Harmonizers used to do. Breaking up families, people disappearing. It was starting again. I might have passed you on the street, and I did nothing. All I had to do was say my name, and maybe I could have stopped this. You wouldn't be in danger again." He sighed, swaying, and I pulled him to the ground, sitting with him. "I don't want to fight anymore, Rowan. I just want to see you home."

He was right. It was time for me to go home, but not to Gran and Grandmother. If the Harmonizers weren't going to keep the city in balance, then I wanted to learn how. Home. That's where change was made. I'd come from the city, and so had Erhent—we could go home again.

He stretched out his leg, blood pooling around his foot. He huffed. "Some legend I am. More like a silly old man stubbing his toe in the dark."

I chuckled, and he started laughing.

"I'm sorry for shouting," he said.

I offered him a handkerchief. "Gran says everyone needs to shout sometimes."

He pressed it against his heel. "Well, have I scared you off toward home?"

"Yes, but not the home you wanted."

He tied off the handkerchief, then leaned back on his hands, his face to the moon. "I know. I can already hear you telling it. A stranger came to town, and that community accepted him with hospitality. When that community was in danger, they worked together to stay safe and keep that danger from others. Two of them went on a quest to find others and warn them. Those two—those two knew they couldn't run away if they truly wanted to help, so they went home."

I squeezed his hand. "One as old as starlight."

Erhent returned the squeeze. "The other as young as a snowmelt stream."

PART III

Plant sequoias.

CHAPTER SEVEN

Why Erhent followed me, some kid who couldn't imagine how fast death can come, I didn't understand other than love. I wanted the hero's stories to be real, to walk with this figure as old as history, to stride into the city and stop the bad Harmonizers, to face them down like he did at the cave. And then every winter at the cave, we'd tell that story. Erhent would come visit from the city or I would go visit him, and he'd show me how everything was healing. I truly believed that's how the story would go. "Maybe it will remember me instead."

At the request of the Archivists, we first headed north over the mountain foothills to the next city, Open Gates. They had emissaries in Haven City and would have advice on how to help those already struggling for change in Haven, since people were surely already organizing. The people of Open Gates traveled to different cities and helped restore them, even those under Harmonizer control. Erhent needed to gather his strength after fighting the Harmonizers who attacked the Archives, so we agreed to take our warning to Open Gates before going home to face the city.

We reached Open Gates four days later, over the biggest hills I'd ever climbed. The clear weather held, and the deeper snow slicked hard enough to walk on. Brother often led the way, picking the least-snowy path. Sometimes, Erhent cleared a trail with his long, slow strides, the snow melting into watery rivulets that twisted away like veins through the brown undergrowth.

After Erhent took back his name, he became even quieter. Maybe it had more to do with winter's softness or his hardening resolve, but I let the quiet stretch and settle. I loved how the snow tamped down the natural noises, and how that made the snap of a stick or the mumble of spoken word that much louder. Some of my favorite memories wintering at the cave were hauling water for tea and the transition from the quiet, snowy woods, the burbling stream, to the chattering cave as all fifty of my family and community packed inside the warm walls. Whenever the voices rose too loud, I'd wrap a wool blanket around my shoulders and snowshoe through the woods, sometimes just for a few minutes and sometimes for hours.

Walking with Erhent felt easy like that, now. Somehow, we'd connected across time. I still believed in purpose—that we could do something to push back the centuries-old forces trying to take too much, like the stories promised. I couldn't let that slip away, not if I wanted to be a storyteller.

Learning how to tell this story felt bigger than just warning others about the advancing city. Erhent had seen so much, and for some reason, a thread of my life had become woven with his. I wanted to understand why. I hoped I might be able to bring the threads together at Open Gates. Cara said we'd have nothing to fear at Open Gates—all kinds lived there, including soulkind. They'd have advice on the city in addition to a radio since it had once been a prison stronghold but had been reclaimed by over ten thousand residents. I'd never been around that many people. When I asked Erhent what it was like, he said it might feel like walking through a dense, thick forest.

Except Open Gates looked nothing like a forest. I had a lot of experience with forests, but the buildings spreading across the valley reminded me of a spider crouched at the heart of a web, waiting. At the top of the last hill, we shared a pair of binoculars. The valley bottom had the cleared look of a place long-poisoned. Most of the nomadic families avoided roads that led to these types of burned-open places in case the poison still lingered in the water or the soil.

I tucked the binoculars into Brother's saddlebag. "Do you think it's safe?"

Erhent crouched and dug his fingers into the frozen ground. After a few minutes, he said, "Yes and no. They've been working on removing the poison, but this place saw more than just pesticides." He sighed. "This place is... wounded. Carrying pain." He brushed off his hands.

"So, can Brother eat the grass?"

"I think so."

The hill descended gently, so we both rode Brother toward the tree-line's end. Towers edged the broken asphalt leading toward the buildings. A too-warm wind whipped through the valley, and no snow remained except in the shadow of tussocks. Winter's brown made the flatlands feel abandoned and dead rather than just resting. Human-projects dotted the land, as did human-made homes for nonhumans. Dead trees piled together near some sort of compost system beside a series of empty trellises. Robins and cardinals darted into the compost and picked at it. Their pinpricks of red loosened my chest.

The first watch tower waited a few miles from where the outbuildings glinted in the weak sunlight. Underneath it, a cement pad supported the legs, and a few young people around my age gathered around the edge, playing some sort of game.

The road passed next to it, and I swung off Brother as we drew closer. The oldest-looking broke away from the crowd and met us at the roadside. They held what looked like a length of wood with wheels attached.

The tallest one waved. Sweat soaked their long shirt. "Hey, on your way to Open Gates?"

I returned the wave. "The Archivists told us about this place. We're here to use your radio and visit your city."

They leaned over slightly, propping on the nose of their board. "You're totally welcome, of course, but the Archives have a radio, don't they?"

Erhent dismounted. "Emissaries from Haven City destroyed it."

They frowned. "What? Hold on, hold on." They turned to the tower and yelled in another language, something that sounded like what the Harmonizers spoke, but not as precise.

A shadow scaled down the tower in long jumps before landing in a crouch.

Erhent stepped beside me but didn't drag me behind him like last time. He clenched his twitching hands behind his back.

"I'm Chasim, any pronoun, and this is Sera, she-her."

The soulkind jogged over. She looked less like the Harmonizers from the Archives and more like Erhent. My height, curvy, with pale skin still tan from the summer.

"We're the welcome duo," Sera said. "So we can give you the talk and tour, but it sounds like there's trouble."

Erhent dipped his head with the stiffness of dead reed. "I'm Erhent." He braced.

Sera tilted her head. "Did you say..."

Erhent tried to smile, ending up more with a grimace, so I did it for him. "Yep! *The* Erhent."

Chasim's board slipped through their fingers and clattered on the asphalt. "Whoa. Uh, welcome."

He waved them off. "We're here because Haven City is expanding."

Sera and Chasim exchanged glances. "First we've heard of it," Chasim said.

"We need to prepare for refugees, then." Sera slipped into the soulkind language, her words sounding like fingers ripping up grass.

Whatever she said helped relax Erhent. "This city doesn't balance?"

Sera made a noise in the back of her throat. "Not in the old ways." She crouched and pressed her hand to the frozen ground. "The work of this city is to pull the hurt and poison from this place. We're only able to support ourselves with the help of all those living around us. Others bring us their surplus, and we give away what we have too much of. I forgot how hardy garlic mustard can be, even in this place."

"Our premiere flavor," Chasim said. He tossed his board onto the crumbling road and stepped on. "C'mon, I'll take you to some of the organizers. They'll know more about this trouble with Haven City."

Despite the broken road, Chasim stayed on the board. They knew the path well enough to make his board jump over the worst sections or to step off, jog, then flip the board back under her feet. Erhent and I swung onto Brother to keep up.

In Uncle Miguel's stories, the cities swooped into tall points, like metal and glass forests, but this city crept along the ground. The towers spiked the flatland, but some stood empty, their joints bending them closer to the ground. Wooden barriers warned away people and larger animals. The city inhabitants had tended other towers, and winter-browned vines turned the structures into shaggy shadows, but still, they felt watchful. Not the good watchful of a lone tree in a wide meadow.

The road cut through a fence still covered in summer's viney leftovers. Chasim popped the board into his hands. "Wish you'd come in summer. Guests never feel as welcome in the winter. We keep this fence because someone long before us planted climbing flowers. It blooms each morning in the summer." She walked beside us where the road turned to dirt and mud. "This place was a mega-prison and then a military stronghold, so it often feels—bad. Oppressive. Newcomers feel trapped or watched. It's usually better once you're at the heart of the city. More peaceful."

I thought it was just the towers making me want to look over my shoulder, even with Erhent riding at my back. In the woods, I usually felt watched, but there was a difference between being watched by a mountain lion or coydog, between a squirrel or a badger. If a city could turn its gaze like this, how did anyone stand to live here?

Erhent touched my shoulder, and I started. "I feel it, too," he said.

"Do they all feel this way?"

"Some. Not all."

I'd felt this wariness, even unwantedness, in places stripped of life. Uncle Miguel once took me to a coal mine a few miles off our summer trails. The gaping hole, the scooped crater, had oozed this same spikiness.

Buildings clustered half a mile ahead, but other human structures spread into the fields. Lean-tos covered hay, and two does munched in the shadow. One raised her head as we passed, and Brother nickered. An earthen structure, the outside decorated with a mural of sunflowers, hunched deep in a flat, empty field. Smoke sputtered from the chimney. More homes clustered at the edges. A solar tractor pulled a wagon across a field while people shoveled compost off the back.

Even in the cold, more people dotted the space. Most paused to wave. Some called to Chasim by name.

"There's about ten thousand humans and soulkind," Chasim said. "And double that in more-than-humans."

I gaped. "What?"

Erhent chuckled. "That's less than a quarter of the size of Harmony."

"But—how does it work? How can so many stick together?"

Chasim grinned. "We just take care of each other."

"There's smaller communities inside the city," Erhent said. "Like parts of a body."

"Or a forest," Chasim said. "Any forest is much bigger than this city."

My face felt hot. "I guess, when you say it like that."

Erhent nudged my foot with his boot. "It *is* a lot of people."

In a few minutes, those people became more and more visible, like seeing one or two wildflowers, then entering the meadow.

So many faces and voices and people doing, doing, doing. Many of the structures stood open, even in the cold, or had big, bright windows. A shop repaired carts and tools, the workers crossing next door to a blacksmith and welding station, where a burly person sharpened a spade. Carpenters offered building materials and decorative wood with intricate patterns burned into the grain—flowers, bees, lines of poetry, a big spread of crows. The carpenters' designs decorated a bakery, which stocked bread on a table outside. People sat to eat and a cat waited for pads of butter. A tea cart rolled up, the driver parking at the bakery. Across the path, a library had e-readers to borrow displayed in the window and a list of current favorite stories pasted to the glass. A pack of dogs slept along the back wall of a steamy laundry. Two people unloaded winter squash from a truck bed, and a horse munched the packing straw. Woods, meadows, and mountains all carried their own smells, but I hadn't experienced anything like the city, a weaving of savory, sweet, wet, smokey, charred.

I slid off Brother onto the stony path. I gasped as I touched the ground. I felt like the fly on the back of a horse. The city twitched around my senses, but when I remained, seemed to settle. Erhent walked barefoot, his boots tied to Brother's saddlebags. He closed his eyes, pressing his toes into the cracks between the stones.

"See what I mean," Chasim said. "Feels different here, right? It's been taking us in, changing. A century of work and at least another to go."

And beyond that, so much more—a learning center where a person taught a class on bike repair to a dozen people of all ages while a crow watched from the signpost overhead. A spicy breath followed three dirty workers as they left a cafeteria. The menu posted on the door read: "winter squash soup, baked hash, and venison." Tomorrow, they'd be serving goat, frybread, and stuffed mushrooms.

Chasim led us through the chaos. He flipped the board under their feet and gave a strong push. Even on the busy path, she swerved into a rhythm as natural as the wind in the trees. A piece of broken cement leaned against the side of the building, and they swung into it, riding up the incline and somehow jumping off as if the piece of rubble had been placed there for him all along.

As she landed and pushed forward, the city seemed to shudder as if releasing a breath. When Chasim jumped a crack, the city breathed with them.

I pointed after Chasim. "Did you see that? That's amazing."

"They're talented," Erhent said. "And the city knows it."

Chasim pointed out her favorite cafeteria and baker, the leather works that had extra boots if we needed new pairs. They helped Brother find a spot at one of the stables dotting the area, and we left him munching on hay with my bags thrown over the stall wall.

As Chasim described the city, its pattern seemed to fall into place. They'd been right about the forest. Just as I knew what to expect around a large oak tree, each part of the city seemed to have the usual clusters. A place to eat, to bathe, to gather, to live, to play. A third of the buildings had been stripped, their bones left to the sky for others to make new homes. Birds darted in and out of brambles or nests tucked into corners.

"This is one of my favorite spots," Chasim said as we turned a corner past a small farm stand offering hothouse tomatoes. The street opened onto a wide space with trees, clusters of oaks and maples, gingkos mixed with hemlocks and firs. Raised garden beds held the remains of summer flowers, and an apiary huddled in a sunny spot. Benches lined the paths, and a group of kids a few years younger than me tossed a disc, their faces red and their breath streaming.

Chasim pointed to a row of buildings that faced the open space. "We'll be in there. Take a moment to catch your breath, yeah?"

I stretched and rolled my shoulders. The city seemed quieter around the open space. "Reminds me of the orchard where I found you."

Erhent smiled. "Let's sit for a moment." He walked to the winter-browned meadow and sat down. After a moment, he fell back and spread his arms.

I crouched beside him. "How's it feel?"

"There's so much pain, rooted deep. But the topsoil is light, joyful." He sighed and settled into the grass.

"Don't fall asleep on me."

He cracked open one eye. "I've told you. I—"

"Don't sleep as much as I think," I said. "I know."

He took a few deep breaths, then rolled to his feet. "Right. Let's go."

We entered the door to the low building. Inside, tables filled a wide room, with smaller rooms off to the sides. People worked at the tables, some on computers like at the Archives. Others talked over mugs. Some looked at a design plan so big it spilled over a table's edges.

Chasim chatted with two others at a circular table. Guessing from Erhent's flinch, at least one of them was soulkind. Chasim introduced Mei and Charlie as half of the ambassadors to Haven City, with their counterparts living in the city. Mei had the long pale hair, white skin, and angular face of the glacial Harmonizers, but her smile held a warmth. Charlie was probably my Gran's age, with gray hair, brown skin, and dark glasses that shaded his eyes. Like the Archivists, Mei and Charlie's partners hadn't raised any alarm or concern about the city growing out of bounds, but on the strength of Erhent's name, they agreed to contact them. Otherwise, all they could do was accept any people in need of a place to stay.

Charlie steepled his fingers. "We do not agree with the city's functioning on—payment, shall we say? But from our understanding, the city remains sustainable, and all are free to come and go. If the system doesn't match with personal beliefs, then that person can leave. We have no reason to intervene."

Erhent sighed. "You're wrong. If the Harmonizers don't want you to leave, they raise the gate price to an amount of calories that would kill the person. At least, that's what they tried to do to me, but I left by other means."

"What do you mean, they'd raise the prices?" I asked. I knew the city required an exchange of energy—even Johnny had mentioned that at the Archives—but stories usually glossed over the specifics.

"In calories," Erhent said. "A balancing for your entrance or exit, but they control the rates." He leaned back in his chair and crossed his arms, hiding his hands. "A gift for the city." Erhent stared at the table.

Mei watched him for a few seconds, then said, "I'm sure you know how soulkind live if you've been traveling with Erhent. It's a give and take, like breathing. We can even filter pollutants out of a place." She touched her chest. "That's part of my work, here. I work in symbiosis with the park outside to remove the toxins from the ground, air, and water." She frowned. "Long ago, there was propaganda that soulkind should feed on humanity to lower the impact on the environment. Most of us fell into the same trap as humanity at that time, that we were the top of the food chain, the chain of being, the most evolved species—however you want to think of it." She nodded at Erhent. "It took elders like him to remind us that's not what predators do."

Charlie eased forward, propping his elbows on the table. "It sounds like the Harmonizers running the city are changing tactics, which aligns with this sudden expansion."

Erhent shoved back his chair. "I—I need to go outside." He hurried out the door, slamming it.

Mei followed and I stood, but Charlie motioned for me to sit. "Let them go, Rowan. Mei can understand his experiences better than we can."

I walked to the wide window. Erhent knelt in a sunny spot at the park's center. Mei crouched beside him.

Charlie joined me. "Will you return to your family now that your task is done?"

I took a deep breath. "I want to go to the city. I want to see this through and help, like you do here." Guilt hollowed my chest. Just me talking about entering the city had upset Erhent. "I came from the city. At least, those are my earliest memories, so I want to go back. I can learn the story and share it."

Chasim glided over, riding his board across the wooden floor. "I want to take a crew to the city. We've taught so many how to skate that Open Gates doesn't need us all. Rowan can come with us."

Charlie chuckled. "I figured you'd say that. Chasim can never turn down a new place to skate." He gripped Chasim's shoulder. "Just make sure you're clear about the risks. The first skateboarders to come here suffered losses, too."

"What do you mean?" I asked.

Chasim popped the board into their hands. "A hundred years ago, the first people to come to Open Gates were skateboarders. We lived here and made it a home long before people like Charlie and Mei took notice."

Charlie huffed. "Not that long. I was born here, remember." "Do you think the city is that dangerous?"

"A healthy city isn't," Charlie said, "but it sounds like this one has become something else in the name of sustainability." He motioned me to follow and stepped to the door, pausing to take two wool blankets hung on a rack. "The hardest lesson we had to learn when working with cities, especially one like Open Gates, is that we couldn't become complacent." He held the door for me, and we sat on a bench outside. Chasim skated past us and around the park, taking long pushes. The city seemed to sigh and settle beneath my feet.

Charlie spread the blanket over his lap. "I don't mean we had to be on watch, but rather we would become comfortable, think we had it all figured out. But this work has to turn like the seasons. It's cyclical, and with the cycle comes change. The moment we tried to lock things into place, thought we had it all figured out, it cracked apart."

Across from us, Erhent and Mei had shifted so they sat cross-legged, facing each other. Erhent leaned back, his hands pressed into the soil, like always. "Is that what you think is wrong with Haven City?"

He shrugged. "I don't propose to know, just giving you my experience."

In the distance, Mei stood and offered Erhent a hand. They walked toward us, still talking. Erhent even laughed.

"Just know, Rowan," Charlie said, "this work is difficult and dangerous. It's good work worth doing, but it's a devotion."

"I want to learn how to do it."

Charlie patted my knee. "Good. We need more folks like you and your friend. But don't be surprised if it's all different than you expect."

✦✦✦✦ ✦✦✦✦

Erhent and I kept exploring. He seemed lighter as we entered a new part of the city. A similar layout meant we knew where to stop for food or drinks. I visited each tea cart to gulp down a steaming cup as the air chilled, but I wanted to see it all. As the sky darkened, lights attached to buildings or wooden poles winked on. The streets quieted, but through the large windows, light illuminated gathering spaces, cafeterias, workshops, a theatre. We paused at a window to listen to a song about two lovers. A person eased open the door and asked if we wanted to come in, but we shook our heads.

A rattling *crack* down the street drew us from the window. Under one of the larger lights at an intersection, a person a few years younger than me rode a board like Chasim's. They circled a small pond with a raised edge and would somehow make the board jump onto the edge, slide along it, then jump off again.

I caught my breath. Beneath the cone of light, the space felt like a stage. The kid could ride the board like a living thing, snaking across the road, gaining speed, riding up a piece of cement leaned against the wall like a ramp. They'd catch the tip of their board on the raised edge of the pond or a bench and hold for a breath before flicking the board back to the ground.

I placed my hand against a building. As before, the city seemed to catch its breath with the kid or maybe the kid skated with the city—or both.

"Do you feel it?" I whispered even though we were far enough away the kid couldn't hear us. "The city likes this."

"Of course it does," Erhent said. "The city and that child are making something beautiful together."

The kid started at the far side of the square, took a running leap on the board, and shoved toward the pond. With so much speed, the kid made it halfway around the lip before levering off. They whooped and stepped off the board, bracing their hands on their knees.

I ran over. "That was amazing!" "Right?!" The kid grinned, all teeth. "The farthest I've ever gotten! Some of the others can get all the way around the lip, but I'm not strong enough for that yet." The kid stomped on the board's tail and flipped it into their hands. "Do you want to try?" The kid held it out.

I nodded. "Are you sure?"

The kid examined the ground, then placed the board so the back wheels rested in a crack. "C'mere, this will help." They showed me where to put my feet. "You can hold my hand if you need to. I'm Altan, but you can call me Alt, they-them." "I'm Rowan."

Alt offered their hand as I placed my left foot over the front wheels and my right foot over the back wheels. The board wobbled like I was trying to balance on a fallen tree, but I gripped Alt's hand. After stepping on and off a few times, Alt showed me how to push.

Erhent sat cross-legged on the pond's edge. He grinned, a real, happy smile I'd only seen once or twice.

After pushing around the square a dozen times, I stepped off the board. My legs quivered. "That's amazing! Thanks for showing me, Alt."

They popped the board into their hands. "C'mon, and I'll introduce you to the others. We can get you a board to use."

I glanced at Erhent, and he nodded. Alt ran down the street, and I followed. The street opened onto another park, but this one had a big, wooden structure at the edge, like two ramps pushed together. Light from a meeting space made patches on the street. Alt banged into the door and shouldered it open, more warm light spilling out.

"Rowan needs a board!" they hollered.

I skidded in after them. About twenty people packed the space, all talking, eating, drinking, and building. Boards and pieces of boards were strewn over worktables. Others packed travel bags with provisions, clothes, and tools.

"Building two now!" someone shouted, and Alt pulled me over to a table.

As Alt's friend Josh taught me how to assemble my trucks, he explained the skateboarders had been asked to go skate Haven City. Skating the city helped map it but also assess the hurt. The joy skating brought had made several break-throughs at Open Gates, so they'd become the first deployed at new locations. And they were proud to be the vanguard. But more than proud—excited. A new place to skate meant new adventures, new tricks, new stories.

They swept me into their preparations, only pausing to show me something about the board they gifted me or to get me different shoes or knee pads or a paintbrush so I could decorate a helmet.

At some point, Erhent tapped me on the shoulder and said he'd be back in the morning. I stayed with the skateboard-ers, sleeping in a part of the old prison. Some of the walls had been knocked out, and everything had been painted in bright colors and decorated with murals or quotes. They had guest beds, but Alt asked if I wanted to sleep in their room, so they dragged in another cot.

Alt talked about how excited they were to skate Haven City until they fell asleep mid-thought. A sliver of moonlight shone through a small window. I tracked it across the narrow room. I wanted to go to Haven City, too, but I worried Erhent was wavering. Maybe if I went with the skaters, he'd feel better about it. He wouldn't stop me if he chose not to go, but I didn't want him to follow me to a place he feared. These skaters weren't afraid—or if they were, they hid it well—but if that place scared Erhent, then it was dangerous.

As soon as the dawn grayed the room, I took the board and crept out. Erhent would be waiting.

He sat on a bench outside, keeping an egg sandwich warm under his coat. I didn't realize how hungry I was until I took a big bite. I tried to speak, swallowed, and tried again: "Where did you go last night?"

"With some of the other soulkind to watch the moon. It was nearly full." He set his foot on my board and rolled it smoothly. "You'll be going to the city with them."

I nodded as I swallowed the last of the sandwich. "I want to."

"Do you still want me to come?"

"Only if you want to. You don't have to protect me this time."

He laughed, but it sounded more like dry leaves rattling. "Haven City isn't like this place, Rowan. It will hurt you, and I won't be able to stop it, not all of it."

CHAPTER EIGHT

This part is familiar to most of you, but it's worth retelling. It's been ten years, after all.

I was fed on for the first time in Haven City. As I stumbled away from the gate guard, clutching the palm-sized metal square that would be loaded with points for the energy that had been taken, Erhent caught me up. He held me tight, and even though I was taller than him, I buried my face in his shoulder.

"I'm so sorry, Rowan. I'm so sorry."

Erhent had warned me and described what it would feel like. I'd given blood before, given my sweat to work—but this, not this. Every muscle in my body locking into place, the feeling of my breath spooling out of me, the burning in my chest, the instant headache. The guard had to hold me upright even though the last thing I wanted was him touching me.

Erhent guided me to a bench along the city wall. Other humans sagged there, but none had someone to comfort them. He eased me onto the bench, and the shooting pains in my legs turned to a dull ache.

He kept an arm tight around my shoulders. "Will you let me help?"

I nodded, and he turned to face me. He gripped my right hand in his and cupped my face in his left. He rested his forehead against mine. "Close your eyes. Deep breath."

As we exhaled, it felt like a cool breeze promising rain rippled over me on a hot, dry day; like peeling off my boots and washing my feet in a mountain stream; like the sunrise waking me after a peaceful night.

I opened my eyes as Erhent raised his head.

"Better?" he asked.

I nodded. The pain and discomfort had faded to soreness, a dull throb. "Thank you." I squeezed his hand.

Erhent stood and dusted off his coat. "I'll be right back." He went to the others resting along the bench. Some accepted his help, but others just recoiled. When he finished, he gripped my shoulder, a tremor in his arm.

He turned his face from where the gate guard watched, joined by another soulkind. "I don't have the energy for this."

"Do you need to rest?"

"There's a park a few blocks ahead."

I walked slowly as he leaned on my arm, even as we both tried to fool the watching guards, acting as if Erhent still comforted me. Concrete walkways guided us toward a park with treetops I could just see above the buildings, the empty branches stretching into the sky. Unlike Open Gates, this city felt quiet, almost dulled, aching. People glanced at me, sometimes smiled, though their gaze slid past Erhent to the ground.

Erhent guided me around a corner, and the park opened between two buildings tall enough I craned my neck. A path cut through the space, with seating on either side. Erhent stumbled to the base of a hemlock and settled underneath it. The branches draped low, half-hiding us.

"Are you okay?" I asked.

He rested his head against the tree and kicked off his boots. "I need a minute."

I leaned next to him, our shoulders barely touching. Here, the city didn't feel hurt like Open Gates. Instead, a hunger licked through my boots and throbbed in my soles, watched me from the roof corners like vultures.

"Do you feel that?" I asked. "It's different than Open Gates."

He pressed his palms to the loam. "It's restless but—hungry. Hungry for more of everything."

After a few minutes, he pulled into a crouch. "Welcome home, kid. Not exactly hospitality."

I shouldered apart the branches as Erhent passed through. "Can we explore? I want to see if I remember anything."

He dusted off his long coat. "Yes, let's walk the city. Well, I'll walk, you skate, see if the city responds."

I unstrapped my skateboard from my pack. "I'm not as good as Alt and the others. The city might not care." Erhent tied the laces and slung the boots over his shoulder. "I think it's the spirit that counts."

We passed onto a concrete walkway and out of the small park. I stepped onto the board. Even though this part of the city was all concrete, asphalt, and tar, Erhent trailed barefoot and barehanded like he walked in the woods. He took his slow, long steps, one hand pressed against the buildings that crowded the street. People stared at him, then seemed to catch themselves watching and wouldn't look again.

To match his pace, I'd push forward to a flat, new piece of concrete and practice jumping the board. Once he passed me, I'd push to him and ease beside him for a few yards, then find another flat spot to practice. The concrete was so smooth and new, I kept braking by sliding my foot across the ground. My shoes would wear thin before long. Maybe the Open Gates crew had a fix. They'd be trickling to the city over the next week, trying to look less like a pack and more like strays.

After my experience at the gate, I didn't expect the city to be so beautiful. Even on this cloudy, winter day, warmth seeped from the buildings. Many of the buildings were painted with bright, fresh colors, signaling spring would come again. Greenhouses on rooftops promised there would still be fresh tomatoes. The sidewalks carried poetry, and murals showed people gardening or wandering in a woodland with the city in the background. Even the sweeping electric lines drew my eye to the next thing, the next mural, the next garden rooftop, the next solar panel mosaic.

Signs, murals, and statues recounted the history of Haven City and told of how Harmonizers had brought peace during different climate wars. The Archives had told the history a different way, and I asked Erhent which was right. Neither told the whole story, he said.

The river ran through the city's center, and even in the chill, people sat on benches and stone walls, sipping steaming drinks or eating boxed lunches. Erhent muttered about the lack of trees, how so many had been taken since he'd left a month ago. Crews spread fresh concrete, and we watched for a few minutes. I'd worked to remove concrete but hadn't seen it poured. As if Erhent guessed my question, he said he wasn't sure why they were making more when plenty of walkways and roads were still uncracked.

We'd seen more construction on our way into the city that morning, and the noise had finally made Brother part ways with us. He kept to the woods around the cave, which hadn't been cleared yet, though a new dirt road had cut through a swathe of the forest.

My first glimpse of Haven City had explained the point of naming a place Open Gates. Walls wrapped around the city, visible from the hills. Parts had crumbled, and dense foliage or metal fencing filled the gaps. The road led to the biggest gap in the wall, with saplings and raised gardens separating people into lines.

We'd passed the morning watching and listening from the last set of hills before coming down into the city's agriculture area, which had been stripped of trees for miles. In the predawn gray, trucks swarmed from a side gate and onto the main road. Through the binoculars, we watched them dig up the paved road, doubling the width. More trucks brought people to the fields. Through the binoculars, it looked like big, yellow machines took bites out of the land.

Tears had filled Erhent's eyes. He'd explained the area around the city had been a woodland. People had come to relax or forage or see the stars. Soulkind would come to rest and restore. What would possess them to cut it all down?

As we'd come from the hills and joined the others walking into the city, a resolve had flowed over Erhent, like shrugging on a familiar coat. Even the night before, he'd asked if I was sure I wanted to go to the city, but now, he led the way.

At a market, signs advertised the day's surpluses—beeswax candles, cherry tomatoes, hard cider—and which new goods had arrived, like fresh hardwood and clay. My favorite streets were packed with restaurants. Using the same basic ingredients, so many options were available. Noodles, sandwiches, salads, grilled meat, fish, rice dishes—I wanted to try it all.

"Anything feel familiar?" Erhent asked.

"Not really." It all felt too new. The buildings tall as trees that Erhent explained were people's homes, the sharp, acrid smells, the vehicles Erhent kept telling me to watch out for (and some instinct warned a boxy black vehicle followed us). The city's weirdness also came from missing things. No birds chirping, no squirrels complaining about my noise, no spiderwebs glittering in the dew. I felt out of place rather than familiarity.

We walked for a few hours and still had more city to see. Like Open Gates, the city broke into sections. Places where people lived seemed separate from the places where people gathered, like markets and libraries and two museums, one for art and one for history. According to my welcome pamphlet, I'd report to the history museum, then the library for an introduction to the city since I hadn't been registered before—an "exchange of energy and knowledge" was how the instructions were worded.

The map on the back of the pamphlet listed sections of the city as "under construction," including the beaches where we hoped to find the Riverroaders. We headed toward the lake, anyway. The temperature dropped, and haze obscured what horizon was visible between the buildings. Before we could see the lake, orange barricades blocked the roads. Metal and wooden sheets covered doors and windows. A sign taller than me read: *Harmonizers and Humans: Building a Better Tomorrow.*

I climbed up one of the barricades, but the setting sun cast shadows between the buildings, the water barely glinting. Machines growled and thrummed, probably closer to the shore. Black smoke trickled over the skyline.

"What do you think happened to the Riverroaders?" I asked.

"Nothing good."

We turned around and followed the map toward a green square labeled Harmony Park. The streets had become busier as long vehicles dropped off people at different corners. Lights flickered in the tall apartment blocks like so many eyes coming awake. Shops opened, and people joined us on the sidewalk.

"It didn't used to be this way," Erhent said. "There's no need to work like this. It's like they have nearly half of the population on some sort of construction crew."

Two oaks spread naked branches over the iron gate to Harmony Park. The small park opened onto a large, tiled plaza, with a fountain in the center, turned off for the winter.

Across the park, a domed building glittered in the sunset. People in city clothes like the Harmonizers wore walked down the tall steps.

Erhent took a quick breath. He swayed and leaned against the gate. "How could they." He stumbled into the park, and I hurried after him. He dropped to his knees where raised concrete marked the beginning of the tiled plaza. He pressed his hands into the winter-brown grass.

I crouched next to him. People, some of them Harmonizers from their paleness and height, stared at us as they crossed from the ornate building into the city. I touched his shoulder. "Erhent?"

"Just like outside the city, the woods. This was a beautiful grove, with old, old trees. Trees that had seen the changes of the centuries. Food trees—walnut and apple and pawpaw trees. Morel mushrooms loved to grow under the apple trees." He pointed toward the fountain. "A cherry tree there produced the sweetest fruit. And there was wild grape growing up the side of city hall." He motioned to the right. "And there, aspens that always sang in the wind. There were birds and a possum family and foxes came here." He pulled himself upright and walked to the fountain. "The idea was that cities should be governed from a green space to remind the leaders and the people of how everything was interconnected."

"There isn't much green left." By the gate, all that remained was a dozen trees, a stretch of grass shorn close.

Erhent shaded his eyes against the sunset glaring off the windows. "I imagine that's the point."

While Erhent struggled to take in the plaza, a group had gathered in the remaining grass. A table built out of stacked crates and a board held platters of food, from the savory smells. A person lifted a sign attached to a broken stick: *Free Food*.

I nudged Erhent and pointed at the gathering. "I'm going to eat. Want some chicory coffee if they have it?"

He passed a hand over his face. "That's not how it works around here. Food isn't free."

"Why not?"

He straightened his coat and took a deep breath. "The Harmonizers say it costs energy to produce it and ship it from the farms outside the city, so you have to pay. That's what you did at the gate." "People have to go through that just to eat?"

"Humans, yes."

We walked over to the group, which had formed a line. Some ate sitting on the grass or leaning against the few trees. Others hurried out of the park as if they'd done something wrong.

"You!"

Erhent whipped around, trying to shove me behind him. A familiar red-bearded person stepped from behind the table and jogged toward us.

I waved. "Brand! You're okay."

Erhent tried to step back as Brand hurried toward him, but Brand caught him in a back-slapping embrace. Erhent grunted.

"You tried to tell us, and I made it all worse." Brand reached over Erhent and gripped my shoulder. "We should have listened."

Erhent ducked away from Brand and smoothed his coat. "Is everyone all right?"

"They took our boats," he said. "We wanted to leave again, go upstream and winter in the valley, but they wouldn't let us. We've been trying to do what we can here."

Another person walked over, younger than Brand but older than me, with black hair braided down the side, contrasting with their pale skin. "Brand, who's this?"

"The ones I was telling you about. The ones who tried to warn us. Eduardo and Rowan." Brand gripped the other's shoulders. "This is Raven. They helped us when we first arrived."

Erhent offered his hand, and Raven gripped his forearm. "I go by Erhent, while I'm here."

Brand sucked in his breath. "Did you say—"

"Holy shit!" Raven smoothed their hands over their hair and down the braid. "You were at the gate today."

Erhent nodded.

"You have to teach me," Raven said. "But, shit, we have to get you out of here, or they'll shut us down."

"Why?" I asked. "What's going on here?"

"With energy rates going up," Raven said, "we've been feeding people, so they don't have to pay the extra for food. But if you can teach us how to do that restoration thing, then we'd make some real change."

Erhent tilted his head. "What do you mean? Nobody taught you how to give?" As Raven tried to explain, a shriek crackled across the park, echoing off the tile and buildings.

"Ah, shit," Raven said.

The black vehicle that followed us around the city had parked at the gate, and two Harmonizers walked through the park. The way they swaggered reminded me of the Harmonizers that had come for my family, killing the trees along the way. I imagined these two might stretch out their hands and claim one of the few remaining oaks.

Raven swore again, but Erhent waved them off. "It's all right."

He met the two Harmonizers away from the group, even though the taller one kept staring at us. A few minutes later, they returned to their vehicle and drove off. Brand let out a long breath.

"What'd you say?" Raven asked.

Erhent smirked. "Oh, just that I, Erhent, heard about their wonderful city and how pleased I was to see humans and soulkind helping each other like nature intended."

Brand gripped his shoulder. "You saved us all getting fined."

"In energy?" Erhent asked.

Raven nodded. "They're trying to wear us down. All our rents just went up, so that's more of our energy, gone. Then they fine us, make it too expensive for us Souls to go out of the city to feed, even if the woods were still there."

The thought of being fed on over and over like that made my chest tighten. "Why don't you just leave?"

"It's my home," Raven said. "I love this place. I don't want to see us all hurting like this."

"We're here to help, if you think we can," Erhent said. While Brand returned to serving food, Erhent explained how more skaters were on their way from Open Gates to volunteer, and how he hoped to use his recognition to influence the older Harmonizers. Raven asked him to first teach them how to give energy back, so Erhent took them to one of the large oak trees to practice.

I stepped onto my board and carved figure eights around the fountain. The anxiety squeezing my chest eased with each glide. Tomorrow, Chasim would arrive with Alt, so I could learn some new tricks.

Once Raven and Brand's group had finished distributing the food, Erhent brought me a plate. We sat together on the edge of the fountain as I stuffed sticky rice balls into my mouth.

"Raven has a place for us to stay," Erhent said. "The visitor quarters are in an expensive tower, so it will save us some energy to stay with them instead."

I nodded. The tightness in my chest returned, and I wrapped up the last rice ball, pocketing it.

Erhent nudged me. "You okay, kid?"

I rested my elbows on my knees and let my hair fall over my face. "I thought I'd know what to do once I got here, but it just hurts. My feet hurt, my chest hurts, being fed on hurts."

Erhent squeezed his hands together hard enough a knuckle cracked. "I should have taken care of this years ago, when I saw the changes coming to the city. But I ran. I knew other soulkind were working with humans to help, but I didn't want to be the hero again. I was just so tired."

I placed my hand over his, and he relaxed. "The other Harmonizers know better. They're choosing to make this harm, so that's why we have to stay here and help. That's what my family taught me to do."

"You're right." He toed the skateboard away from me. "Others have already been working hard to balance that pain." He stood and easily stepped onto the board. "We have to remember, we aren't working alone." He pushed the board forward, set his feet, and jumped.

The board rotated under his feet.

"What!" I shot off the fountain. "You—you never said! That's so unfair!"

He grinned. "It's the only trick I know, I promise. I'll teach it to you tomorrow."

I ran after him. "No way, right now! Show me again."

***

The second time I was fed on was a fine for skateboarding. That's when Erhent joined the Harmonizer council. While I skated, Erhent worked with the local organizers who had been protesting the energy hikes since they began two years ago. Most of the soulkind were very young, as it seemed elder soulkind either believed in the city expansion or had left the city. Erhent taught them how to give energy back to those who had been fed on. He kept himself replenished by walking the city at night, trailing, just like he would when we traveled. Usually, I'd skate with him until my legs wobbled or

I couldn't stop yawning. He'd walk all night sometimes, but it didn't seem to be enough. He looked more worn, even as held tight to the hero the stories claimed him to be.

Compared to the soulkind that chased me down and shoved me off my board, Erhent looked less like a returning warrior and more like a storyteller retired by the fire.

I hit the sidewalk, rolling off my shoulder and onto my skinned knees. The Harmonizer hauled me upright. They were pale as the new concrete with shaved white hair signaling this Harmonizer was one of the glacial soulkind. The propaganda for the city said no hierarchy existed, but since any soulkind could claim a human was "out of balance" and take from them, that didn't hold true. The glacial soulkind were the most likely to cause trouble for humans as opposed to soulkind like Erhent and Raven, who hadn't come from the melting glaciers and often supported humans.

The kids I'd been teaching how to skateboard had been smarter than me and took off the moment this soulkind had turned the corner. At least they had the boards I'd given them. If they had the courage to keep practicing, I'd find them again.

The Harmonizer shoved me against the wall of an apartment building. "Sign says no skateboarding." They ground the heel of their hand against my skull. "Fine is one thousand calories, but you tried to run away, so I'm going to double it."

I braced as it felt like all the strength in my legs, my back, my chest was ripped through a tiny hole in my skull.

The soulkind left me gasping, sitting against the building. They reached for my skateboard caught on the curb, but it almost seemed like something twitched in the concrete, and the skateboard rolled off, across the quiet street. The soulkind sneered and kept walking.

I hid my head between my knees, my fingers buried in my hair. At least I still had my board. Wasn't the first time it seemed like the city turned in our favor. Chasim swore an alley entrance opened where he didn't remember one. Alt saw a Harmonizer trip on what was perfectly new concrete seconds before. Other skateboarders talked about a similar response to what they'd felt in Open Gates: the perfect stairway to jump or railway to grind; a piece of construction material leaned at the right angle for a mini-ramp; jumping a random orange cone left behind.

This was the first time the city had opened for me, after a month of skating. A tightness made me take long, slow breaths. If I didn't get something to eat, I felt like I'd pass out. I for sure wasn't strong enough to walk back to our squat, but food cost energy, just like the bus.

Something smacked the wall next to me, and I tensed, hunching my shoulders. A protein bar, dented at one corner, set on the sidewalk a few feet away. I glanced up, and a person waved from the apartment building across the street. They flashed a thumbs up, and I returned the gesture before tearing into the paper wrapper.

At least I still had my board. I hurried across the street, paused to stretch out a calf cramp, then glided down the sidewalk. The sidewalk seemed extra smooth.

I made it to the park in front of city hall. Even though it was supposed to snow that evening, we'd planned a skate session by the fountain to protest the skateboarding fines. The city council had passed the ruling two weeks after we arrived, which was the best sign we were making some sort of change even if it made our jobs harder. At least, that's what Chasim said.

I walked the final blocks to the park, hoping Erhent hadn't arrived yet or was already busy passing out food or helping with restorations. I didn't want him to see me so weak, watch the guilt flash across his face.

Good for me, he was surrounded by humans and soulkind, but the second he noticed me, he hurried over.

I tried to wave him off. "I'm fine, just need to eat."

He gripped me by my shoulders. "What happened?"

I shrugged. "Skateboarding fine."

"Look at me."

I rolled my eyes but looked down at him. He must have already been giving to several people. His bright eyes had dulled.

"I said I'm fine."

"They took too much."

"That's the whole point."

He offered his hand, palm up. "Let me—"

"Others need you."

"Well, I wouldn't be here without you."

I stepped around him and hopped onto my board. "I said, I'm fine." I did a kickflip like he taught me. "See?"

He sighed and walked beside me. "We can't keep this up. Chasim got fined, too. Even the younger ones were fed on, and they should be exempt." He nodded at the glittering building. "But the rule makers can break their own rules. Always been that way."

"Then we're fucked at the skate session tonight."

He smirked. "You've been hanging out with Raven, I see."

"They wanted to learn to skate."

"We can't keep this up—and just when we were making progress. Reports are the city likes it. Little responses like they're used to seeing at Open Gates."

We paused where the grass became concrete tiles around the plaza. Half a dozen people from Open Gates worked with a few community members, teaching them how to step on a board, showing more advanced learners how to ollie.

"Well," Erhent said, "I guess I should try making some rules." He walked toward the city hall steps.

I pushed my board, catching up to him. "Wait, what are you doing?"

"Taking a seat on the city council whether they like it or not." He paused on the first step and took a deep breath. "They won't say no to Erhent."

CHAPTER NINE

W e lived in Haven City for a year. Erhent openly used his name, forced his way onto the city council, and gave all the energy he could spare to replenish what the other Harmonizers took. He taught others how to give while I taught people how to skate.

The city council made it illegal for the soulkind to give energy to humans, but Erhent dissented, blocking the ruling. With Erhent on the council, we thought we'd found a way around them, but after a few weeks, they banned him by charging him with criminal acts from his past, even if those same acts—destroying dams, helping people cross borders, stealing from the trillionaires—are what made him a legend in the first place.

We fought in the streets, too. Raven and Brand organized protests while the Archivists based in the city printed pamphlets and made videos that told alternate histories to what the Harmonizers claimed was the truth. The Open Gates skaters played in the city's veins. We learned every rail, every stair, every crack, and felt the city purr beneath our wheels.

But still the people went hungry, and the city stretched for more, more, more, even though we all would have enough if the Harmonizers would only truly believe in balance. So, the city spread, and we all had to help it spread or else we'd starve, too. Starve or give up or run. But not everyone could leave. Why should we just because we had that privilege?

At night, I'd go trailing with Erhent if I wasn't too tired. He'd walk the city until dawn, sometimes teaching other soulkind how to breathe with the city and filter out different pollutants.

Tonight, he said he wanted to talk and asked me to come with him, alone. We'd just had a protest go bad, with people hurt. One of the skaters had nearly died, and it was only Erhent and Raven working together, pouring all the energy they could into the skater, that saved them. Like Chasim and the others, I could only wait and watch, feeling like a fish trapped at a dam. But what else could we do?

Now, just the two of us, we came to the park by the gate where we'd first rested a little over a year ago. The park had been slated for construction—another apartment building—but we'd skated the area all day and night, without a break, until the city council finally backed off. One of a handful of victories among a bucket of failures.

Erhent lifted the hemlock's branches so we could sit against the trunk, hidden by spreading boughs. He eased down with a long sigh. This year had rubbed him raw. Even the others could see it and asked if he was okay. More gray streaked his black hair, and his eyes dulled, even after a night of trailing. His thin frame had grown angular, and his coat hung loose off his shoulders. Thankfully, I'd grown taller, rangier, and I still felt strong, even though it seemed like I took the brunt of the fines—another way to target Erhent.

He patted the ground beside him, and I sat down, my board balanced on my knees.

"You okay?" I asked.

He rubbed at the scars along his jaw. "This is just like before, Rowan. Have we learned nothing?" He pressed his head against the bark and closed his eyes. "They don't care because any imbalance won't hurt them. Even if the whole city turned against the Harmonizers, we'd be no match for their power. I can't fight like that, not again. But what else is there? To wear ourselves into oblivion? Then they win. Should we make one final stand? Then they win." He opened his eyes, but they didn't brighten like usual. "I'm just making you a target, our friends a target."

"Don't worry about me. I'm—"

He shook his head. "A hero is just someone to be defeated."

I fiddled with the skateboard wheels to keep my foot from tapping. "You've made things better." I'd given him this speech twice before. When we came back hurt, swaying on our feet, when the energy rates went up again, he'd wondered if we were taking the wrong path. "It's not so hard, now, with so many soulkind helping keep us all strong. You taught them that. And the city likes the skateboarding. It's not so bad when we're skating and having fun."

He looked at his hands, palms up in his lap. "I can't keep doing this. I know what will happen. To keep me quiet, they'll take you, or one of the others. Or they'll threaten to raise energy rates again. They'll just keep coming. That's how the story goes." He thumbed one of the skateboard wheels, and it still spun smoothly. "Yes, there are small victories, but the larger narrative, it ends here. A polluted city, a starving people, a shell-blasted world."

"We'll write a new one. Together. We can fight them, Erhent."

"Fight them." He laughed, the edges hard. "Even I can't fight them, anymore. I told you that, Rowan."

"Then—then you don't have to. I'll just tell your story, and we can act in your name. You inspire people, all of us. We need you!" My voice cracked.

"I can't be part of this story, Rowan. This is your world, your home. I'm just a stranger come to town."

I shot to my feet, knocking aside the skateboard. "Stop it. You're not a stranger. You're part of my family."

He shushed me and tugged at my arm until I sat again. "You said it when we first met. All stories are about love. You love this place, and you love skateboarding, and you love wintering in the woods, and the paths your family travels. So love this place and these people, don't live out of anger." He tucked his arm through mine. "I don't have the strength to live this way. You think you do, that's youth, but if we are just going to keep fighting a battle we can only lose, that's playing the hero in their story. I've lived that story so many times. And what other stories are forgotten in the process?" He spread his hand next to mine, both our knuckles scarred, our skin rough and cracked. "Tell me, Rowan, how do those stories end, those old legends about me?"

"You lost, in the end. We all lost. But this world isn't so bad, Erhent. It's not what you fought for, but I love it."

"Exactly. Never give up. But different worlds need different stories. Not stories of fear and anger. Live a love story. See how that changes the city."

I swallowed hard. "Why are you talking like you won't be here. You can't leave. We need you—"

"I need to rest." He tilted his head toward the stars hidden among the branches. "Deep rest."

My voice broke. "I need you. I can't do this without you."

"But you can't do it with me, either." He shrugged off his long coat and folded it. "I'm just resting, Rowan. I'll still be here. I'll be able to sense you skating, and you can come tell me the new stories you learn." He handed me the coat. "Keep this safe for me. I'll be back for it. And you."

I clutched the coat to my chest. "Erhent, please."

"I followed you to this city even when I wanted to run over the mountains and keep going. I need you to trust me, just like I trusted you."

He settled against the trunk, his legs straight and loose. He offered his hand, palm up, and I gripped him tight.

"Tell me a story, Rowan."

I felt him fall into the city, like skating downhill, the speed wobbling my board, like flying.

CHAPTER TEN

Ten years ago, we started telling different stories. We let Erhent return to legend, except for his teaching moments. Soulkind went to his tree to learn how to rest and pull the hurt and pain from the starving city. The council tried to remove him as more people gathered, but the city wouldn't let them, and we keep a close eye on him. He's resting, but it's also restoration.

We humans learned from Erhent, too—no more heroes, no more sacrifice, lay the legends to rest. When one of us became the focus, became too popular so we felt the Harmonizers drawn to us, we rested. We passed the work to another.

We devoted our days to feeding each other, holding each other close. Our message became—no one starves. And once the people were fed, we gave our time meeting other needs, skating, telling tales, having fun.

And when the people were fed, the city stopped starving. No longer a trapped animal stretching for a scrap of meat, the city's hunger settled. We told stories to explain how the city wanted to feed the starving people struggling in its streets, wanted to feed them just as much as we had, so the city stretched and grew and expanded. Except that wasn't the answer when the only thing keeping the people hungry were those running the city. The city hadn't needed more space to feed its people, it had needed different leaders.

As we worked to keep our communities housed and fed, the Harmonizers' power slipped. Erhent's rejection and rest moved some to come talk with people like Raven, so more and more learned how to give back rather than just take and take. With Erhent diffused into the city, some simply left for grander places. Other elders said the city whispered in their dreams that they had been in the wrong, that it was time to let the old ways go.

Even so, plenty still clung to the title of Harmonizer. We've been fed on lots since then, but now, there's always a soulkind willing to restore, even right there, in the moment. If they can't threaten us with weakness, if there's always someone to aid, then all they can take from us is our lives—and we won't let that happen. There's more of us than them, and the city likes our skating, our art, our stories told late at night while we're walking the streets, laughing.

A few years later, my family moved to the city. Granmum and Grandmother were finding the road troublesome rather than enjoyable, and, even with some of the youngins they'd picked up along the road, they felt their time and knowledge better given to the city than kept in the woods. They worked with the architects to design multi-species spaces, like their favorite places from their many travels. They taught any who wanted to learn how to forage in the returning woodlands surrounding the city. Uncle Miguel settled into the libraries like he'd always dreamed of doing, learning and reading and practicing his storytelling. On the long winter nights, he told us the new stories he'd gathered about how humans and soulkind learned to live together, their different ways of restoring the world making a harmony. Octavia always wished the city would be free of the Harmonizer's hierarchy, so she joined in the work with me, and I taught her how to skate. Even Brother returned and lived outside the city for a few years, helping the woodland regrow.

Every day, I skated the paths Erhent liked to walk, and I felt him, like a ripple. Sometimes, I caught his reflection running with me as I glided past shop windows, or his shadow would jump a curb alongside me. I still tell him stories. Him and the other soulkind that come to help and rest with him. They stay for a few days, months, sometimes a year. Erhent's legendary name draws them, but they all learn from his resting.

Tonight, on the solstice, I always tell this story so new people coming to the city will know what we learned with Erhent ten years ago. We don't fight the Harmonizers; we keep ourselves fed, housed, and laughing. When we hold each other up, we thrive.

EPILOGUE

The city's wall came down piece by piece, as needed. Some chunks became paving stones, some made garden dividers. Others built shelters and lean-tos. The smoothest pieces became skate pads.

Life skittered through the gaps in the wall. Crickets sawed from window boxes. Squirrels made homes in the new street trees. Redwing blackbirds whistled along the pond designed to filter rainwater in the park. Trout and bass returned to the river, and soulkind rested with their feet in the shallows while humans ran the rapids in city-made kayaks.

Framed by the gaps in the wall, the returning woodland bloomed with purple cone flowers, white daisies, violet lupins. Dandelions lined the walking paths and milkweed swayed in the warm breeze. Saplings shaded mossy hollows and streams, now dry until a heavy rain or next spring's snow melt. Apple, peach, pear, and cherry trees clustered near the broadest paths, paved with that crumbling wall, so generations would eat and drink well. Soulkind trailed through the meadow, usually joined by foragers or gardeners who loved to watch the land bloom. When the weather shifted too abruptly or the rain took too long to come, soulkind could usually be found resting between the saplings, helping them stay strong. Children yell *thank you* as they peddled by on bikes.

Rowan stands beneath what had once been the gate's arch, the only piece left. Someone had painted on the keystone: *Nobody Starves*. Even though the symbol of the gate and all the pain it had absorbed was gone, so much work remained that Rowan's chest ached. The council still clung to power, a new soulkind faction was rising, something had poisoned the nonhumans in the lake last summer, a spring blight meant more winter fields needed to be planted—and, and, and. But today, Rowan isn't thinking about those troubles.

Today, Rowan carefully holds a coat, folded twice, the collar arranged just so. A hand shades Rowan's eyes. Down the road, people work the woodland, human and soulkind, but none make Rowan move. Rowan's foot jitters a skateboard, clacking the wheels on the road, as if searching for the right moment to fly.

A shift in the air, a twitch in the asphalt, makes Rowan turn around.

"Hey, kid."

Rowan leaps toward Erhent and catches him up in a hug ten years in the making. "Can't call me kid anymore, huh." Rowan flexes just enough to lift him to his toes.

He looks so much *better*. Strong, standing tall, his eyes bright and his black hair, grown long, pulled back. His scars have faded to the barest lines.

He reaches up to grip Rowan's shoulders. "I'm so proud of you. I watched all that you did."

Rowan's grin is so wide it hurts. "I know. I felt you there. I know you helped me out that one time I was running after skating that stairwell by the lakeshore."

Erhent's grinning, too. He laughs, and it's light and airy. "Well, after you landed that jump, I had to make sure you made it back safe."

Rowan offers him the coat. "You look really good. Less worn."

He slips into the sleeves. The coat is a little tight across the shoulders now. "I'm no longer starving in an apple orchard, if that's what you mean."

They face the road and the woodland beyond. Erhent stretches an arm around Rowan's shoulders, even though Rowan is almost too tall. "So, we aren't strangers, and I think I'm done with quests."

"Oh, I've learned all new types of stories, now. I've got loads to share with you." Rowan points past the city, over the hills that slowly grow into mountains. "Let's walk that way, and I'll tell you my stories, and maybe we'll gather some new ones along the way."

ACKNOWLEDGMENTS

Thank you to Justine Norton-Kertson and Android Press for giving this project a home and space to take root. A big thanks to Brianna Castagnozzi for the amazing cover art bringing the characters and world to life.

Thank you to G. W. Hawkes, whose ideas on storytelling were the seed of Rowan's character.

Thank you to David Anthony Durham for his feedback and to his fiction workshop at University of Nevada, Reno in the fall of 2019—you all gave me the courage to keep working on this project. A special thanks to Naseem Jamnia, December Cuccaro, Leanne Howard, and Andy Butter for all the support over the years in Reno and for your feedback on these characters.

Thank you to Cameron Gibson, a true friend. I wrote all of this novella on your laptop.

Thank you to my husband, Andrew Dincher, for always encouraging me, championing me, and giving me the time to write.

And finally, thank you to my family, who read my first stories almost two decades ago.

ABOUT AUTHOR

Phoebe Wagner's debut novel *A Shot of Gin* is forthcoming from Parliament House Press (2023). She is the editor of three solarpunk anthologies, including *Sunvault: Stories of Solarpunk & Eco-Speculation*. She blogs about speculative literature at the Hugo-winning *Nerds of a Feather, Flock Together*. Wagner currently pursues a PhD, studying eco-criticism and speculative fiction at University of Nevada, Reno. She is an Assistant Professor of Creative Writing at Lycoming College in Pennsylvania. Follow her at phoebe-wagner.com or on Twitter: @pheebs_w.

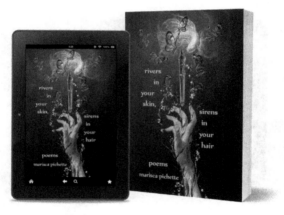

CAGED OCEAN DUB
Glints & Stories

DARE SEGUN FALOWO

Coming June 20, 2023

Pre-Order at
www.android-press.com/bookstore